'This is a terrifically atmospheric page-turning adventure told through words and comic art... it's a rattling good read and one in which you are sure to be drawn in to Jemima's exploits of survival.' – *Lovereading.co.uk*

'Through pace and narrative power, both admirably sustained, the book avoids becoming didactic. This is no campaign document on climate change... The characterization, especially of Jemima and Nick, is forceful and convincing. They capture the reader's interest and carry the narrative forward...' – *Armadillo Magazine*

'Robin Price's writing is quirky with a bit of an edge to it that greatly adds realism to this dystopian version of London... Add in the gritty illustrated comic panels by Paul McGrory and you find this is indeed something quite new, not only in plot, but in style... Children aged 9 and above who are reluctant to read but love comics will find the shorter full text sections easy to get through, with the comic panels adding punctuation to the action occurring within that part of the chapter.' – *Dooyoo.co.uk*

'Is this part graphic novel, part standard text, or is it a story with illustrations...? ... My eleven year old loved it and seemed to have no trouble cutting backwards and forwards between the two...' – Rachel Ayers Nelson, *School Librarian Magazine*

'London Deep is a really amazing story about a twelve year old girl called Jemima Mallard. She lives in a flooded London of the future!! ... This book is a very enjoyable read with lots of drama action and fun. The comic pics are very enjoyable to look at and they fit well with t ... ted 10)

LONDON DEEP

MOGZILLA

London Deep

First published by Mogzilla in 2010

Paperback edition:
ISBN 13: 9781906132033

Story & concept copyright © 2009 Robin Price
Artwork copyright © 2009 Paul McGrory
Cover by Rachel de Ste. Croix
Cover copyright © Mogzilla 2009
Copy editor: Mogzilla
Printed in the UK

www.mogzilla.co.uk/londondeep

www.paulmcgrory.co.uk

Paul would like to thank the following people:

Rachel, Jim, Carol, Kathy, Jane Stobard, Graham, Bob &
Elizabeth, Adam, Debbie, Joseph, Paul, Clarky and the Boy
Jack.

Robin would like to thank the following people:

Scarlet, Mum and Dad, Michele, Peter, Rachel, Alex, Susie
Q, Tegan, Matt, The Chariot, Christina, Sam, Phil, Rupert,
Nic, Ed, Jon, Olivia, George & Kate.

Backwater

THE RADIO SAID THE PRICE OF AIR WAS GOING UP AGAIN.

Then it died. Jem decided there was nothing on the news worth winding the radio up for anyway. Luckily, she'd just been given three tanks of air for her birthday. That was really generous for dad. He'd told her to make it last. Now she was twelve years old, Jem had decided it was time to start listening to her father. However...

The *Advanced Police Diving Manual* said there were only five dangerous species of fish in the river Thames. None of them were sharks. Clearly the shark hadn't read *The Advanced Police Diving Manual*. Jem wasn't taking any chances, so she kicked for the surface. When she hauled herself aboard her boat in the fading light, there was no wind. So she had to get the oars out and row.

On the way home she'd been blown off course. It was easy to lose your way with the river winding through the marshes. She remembered drifting around here with Abel – her first boyfriend. They loved shouting at each other. He was the one who'd nicknamed her 'Miss Hap' because she never seemed to be happy. In the end, he'd chucked her – off a pier. That had been his first mistake.

With a scrape of timber on metal, the boat came to a sudden halt.

In a panic, Jem realised that she'd been rowing straight towards a restricted area. The water was dark and cloudy, not the normal clear Thames blue. To warn off passing boats, the 'Dult police had put a huge ring of buoys around the danger area. Their sign said: CRIME SCENE, STAY OUT!

Not to be outdone, the Youth Police Department had also taped off the whole area with their trademark wasp-stripe tape. Jem didn't get it. If the murky water inside the 'black holes' was poisoned, couldn't it just flow out and mix with the rest of the river? The cops had put a few ropes around the polluted area. Like that would make a difference! Pointless, but both forces liked everything done by their books. Peering out across the ripples, Jem saw that the black hole wasn't actually black. It was a more of a murky brown colour, like one of her dad's Yorkshire stews, and just as mysterious. A white swan made an ugly landing, clipping the rope with its back legs as it flopped into the water. With a sudden grace, it turned in a swanly manner and pecked at a bit of drift wood. Swans are incredibly fussy birds, thought Jem. If this water is clean enough for swans...

Strangetown

BACK ON HER HOUSEBOAT, JEM SIPPED MISO SOUP FROM A MUG WITH AN APD LOGO ON IT. Her dad had told her off once for leaving soup sludge at the bottom of his mug so Jem had made it a tradition ever since. As she drank the soup, Jem thought how ironic it was that the police would steal mugs from their own canteen. Dad said it was impossible to stop it. Stuff slipped off the station boats like water off a duck's back. *The Strangetown* was as quiet as a creaky old boat can get, except for the tick-tock-ticking of the tiger clock in her cabin. It was stripy and one of the hands looked like a tiger's tail. It was weird the way that clocks got louder and quieter. Sometimes you could barely hear them beating out time, sometimes each tick scratched your brain like rats on the cabin roof. Suddenly, she heard an unfamiliar sound:

WHAT'S THAT?

From somewhere out on the open water came the buzz of a small engine, a jetski most likely. Jem didn't think about reporting it. Secretly she liked engines, even though they were illegal. There was something about the whine of an exhaust that whispered excitement. Engines were interesting, it was too bad that they polluted the river.

Jem went over to the window to take a look. *The Strangetown* was more house than boat and never left its mooring at Trafalgar Swamp. Low water, when the tide was all the way out, was still two hours away. But already you could see the first Mayor's great head sticking up out of the water. Little blue waves kissed his broken nose.

'Wack!' called a duck that had appeared from nowhere. It pecked at the Mayor's ear, which was all slimy with weed.

'Wack!' it called again. Jem wondered if it was her imagination, or was the duck speaking to her?

'Wack! Wack! Wack!'

'I think you need to work on your conversation skills,' said Jem.

One of Jemima's earliest memories was of feeding a family of ducks, that had made their home near where *The Strangetown* was moored. That was back in the day when Jem's mum and dad were still together. She must have been about three years old.

Ever since that fateful finger incident, Jem had hated ducks. And this one was no exception.

'Peck off!' yelled Jem, pounding on the glass.

'Wack?' called the duck. 'Wack, wack?'

'Move! There's nothing for you, greedy.'

But the duck wasn't going anywhere.

'Wack!' it called again. Then Jem had a thought. She tore off a chunk of her birthday cake. Dad had made a big fuss about baking it with his own two hands. Jem had told him it was yummy, but in fact it was too dry. Now the icing had solidified like concrete. Unlocking the window, she waved the cake at the duck.

'Come on then,' she cooed, in a voice like chocolate sprinkles. The duck cocked its head and paddled closer. Jem threw the lump of cake straight at its head. Her dad's baking hit the water with force.

'Scram!' she shouted, already regretting throwing the cake so hard. But water runs off a duck's head as easily as its back. It dipped its head into the water and began to gobble up the floating pieces. Suddenly, the howl of a jetski broke the calm.

A wave from the ski crashed over a sign saying 'Slow down – wakes cause damage!' The duck bobbed over this wave, and began to search for cake again. The jetski made another pass – closer to *The Strangetown* this time.

Jem caught a glance of the youth on the back of the ski. He was shouting and waving a weapon over his head. On dry land, he'd probably be strutting about in celebration. He kissed the badge on his t-shirt and held it towards her. Jem could just make out the letters C.F.C, on a blue background. Then he killed the motor and floated – waiting for her next move.

Jem ran from the window and hit the 'panic' button. A powerful spring released a catch. Metal shutters snapped down in front of the windows. Once she was sure that they were shut tight, Jem rushed to the galley. The radio was in the fridge, where she always kept it, but it was dead. A note stuck to the radio said: 'I'm your friendly radio, so wind me up before you go!

Jem ripped up the note and began winding the radio frantically. Two minutes later, a green light on the dial blinked weakly. Jem stabbed the talk button three times. Through the static hiss, a round sounding voice said: 'C.Q.D.X. Identify yourself?'

A strange sucking noise carried across the airwaves, not unlike the sound of lips on a lollipop.

'This is Bravo, Alpha, Bravo, Yellow,' sighed Jem.

Apparently, someone at the police station got a kick out of making up silly call signs for Jem that spelled words like 'B.A.B.Y' or 'K.I.D.D.O.' They were changed every few weeks as a security measure. It was tough being 'Frogspawn' – a cop's kid. You got a heap of fill from the normal kids, and another helping from the Youth Police – so you didn't need it from the 'Dult Police as well.

14

Although she'd known Jem since the girl was a toddler, Sergeant couldn't swing the APD into action. The jetskiers were the YPD's problem. But she promised to send a launch to pick Jem up and to keep Chief Inspector Mallard posted too. 'He's with top brass now. Probably taking some biscuits into custardy.'

As the daughter of a Chief Inspector in the APD, Jem had seen her father chug on merrily through all sorts of situations. Okay, she was more than a bit scared right now, but she wasn't about to let it show. She thanked Sergeant and grabbed her diving kit and the precious air. Then she threw some clothes into her waterproof duffle bag. The second seal was a bit of a struggle – she almost ripped as she tugged it shut. The packing frenzy came to sudden halt as Jem stood gazing at the tiger clock for an age before finally deciding to pack it. This meant another struggle with the seals on the duffle. This time the dodgy seal broke. Furious, Jem pulled the contents out of the duffle and stuffed them into her Dad's floatsack – a long flat rucksack with a float inside. Dad never used it, he was 'sailing a desk' these days.

Jem loved her old tiger clock, even if the book she was reading said it was important to be able to let go of things at the right moment.

She hoarded 'treasures' like a magpie, her cabin was full of them. Her father didn't approve. Whenever he said, 'Stuff is for shallows,' she'd reply: 'That's really deep, Dad.' Secretly, she was starting to agree with him. There'd been too much stuff before the flood, according to her history tutor Mrs. Shah. Jem loved history and had read a lot of the pre-flood stories. They were mostly fairy tales. But there were also grim tales of kids younger than Jem stabbing each other. The media had sent them mad, Mrs. Shah had reckoned.

Jem had practiced for emergencies so she knew what she was supposed to do. The rule book was heavy, with print too small to read in a crisis – as Jem had pointed out. To sum up the 602 pages, in case of trouble you should stay with your boat. Unfortunately, every wannabe Captain Kidd on the river also knew the rules. A sudden blast set the old boat rocking.

16

Every window and cabin was fitted with heavy wooden shutters, but strong oak wouldn't hold off intruders for long. The other option was to slip off *The Strangetown* unnoticed. Old wooden barges weren't built with escape hatches. But Jem's dad had fitted one at the stern. He'd hidden it behind a couple of dummy solar panels. 'Remember to give it a proper kick,' he'd said.

The water was just as cold as she'd expected. So cold, it made her gasp. Searching for her bearings, Jem spotted Ken's Column, lit up like a red Christmas tree, to warn passing ships. Now she'd got her bearings, Jem swam underwater with powerful strokes, building up the speed with her kick. Jem was a good swimmer, but the Thames was immeasurably strong. When its currents got hold of you, they could drag you anywhere. After two minutes of hard strokes, Jem dared to rise to the surface. Catching her breath, she scanned the horizon and soon spotted the red glow of the lights of Ken's Column. Breaking another rule, she risked a glance back towards her boat. Jem was half expecting to be spotted by the intruders and followed. Even she couldn't outswim a jetski. But what she saw was far worse. In the midst of the boiling mass of water, *The Strangetown* was dancing a terrible jig.

Jem had seen the Thames get rough before, but this was wilder than any winter gale. Its wooden back broken, *The Strangetown* gave up the struggle and began to roll over. Jem had no time to watch it slip away. Instead she fixed upon the huge waves that were ripping towards her like ripples from a giant's skim-stone. Thinking fast, she unhooked the straps of her float-sack and reversed it, so it was now under her belly. As she struggled to do up the straps, she was forced upwards on the first of the great swells.

By the time the APD arrived in their launch, the jetski kids and *The Strangetown* were both long gone. The river was calm now. A seagull flying overhead might have looked down and seen a dark circle, like a giant muddy spot in the middle of the river – with the old column on its outer edge. But there were no seagulls. The only bird on the river was a small white duck. It held itself in mid stream, battling the current. Then, with a splash, it turned in a neat circle and began to follow the APD launch on its way up river towards the Station Boat.

Outboard

Jem woke up to a terrible howling. With a crash, her tiger clock parted company with the wall. She picked it up with a curse and then gave herself a silent telling off for cursing so much. Police cells weren't designed with clocks in mind. Sticky tape slid off the metal walls. This cell had been converted into 'police accommodation', which basically meant putting a handle on the inside of the door and removing the cameras. Someone had started to paint the walls cream but they'd given up. Home sweet home!

Few traces of The Strangetown had been found, apart from some pans and a bag of dirty laundry, so Jem was living on the station boat again till they got a new houseboat. It was probably for the best, as her dad had put it, because the youths may have recognised her (and might even have been coming after her for some random reason). So it meant a new home, a new school – in short, the usual. The real shame was that it also meant new friends. Or these days, no friends. Till it was all sorted, she'd be kicking her heels around the station boat. 'Owwwoooo!' bayed Jem, doing a good imitation of a police dog at breakfast time. 'Oooowwwwooo!' The dog chorus howled back at her.

With any luck, she was annoying the rest of the station. If they had seen fit to give her a room opposite the police dog section, that was their own lookout. She grabbed her diving suit and wound the handle. Finally, the cell door began to slide open. The corridor was covered in dark wood and smelt of cabbage. Probably bilge in the bio loos again. Jem leapt up the series of ladders like an old hand but spoiled the effect when she scuffed her head on the hatch. As she emerged, the boat was gently rocking with the retreating tide. Sergeant was propping up the reception desk as usual.

Like the shutters on *The Strangetown*, the station boat's doors were on a powerful spring so that they could be snapped shut in an emergency. The downside was, you were forever winding the cursed things up.

Outside, the light bounced off the white roofs of the boats, making the blue of the river even more perfect. Every roof in London had been painted white, from the Barrier Reef to the Watford Isles. The scientists had insisted on the white-wash as they said it would reflect sunlight back into the sky. It might slow global warming, but keeping the things clean was a drag. Half of them were under water now.

Jem made her way to the air store. A pair of swans had made their nest on a blue APD launch, which sported a water cannon at the front. There wasn't any call for an old-fashioned riot boat these days. But the APD kept it ready just in case. It was Jem's dad who'd saved it from the Great Recycle. Mallard loved old machines with real engines – even if you could only fire them up once a year.

It was only a short step around the jetty towards the air store, a metal storage shed where Jem had left her air tanks. Looking forward to a morning's diving, Jem wound at the door handle. Then she was interrupted by a growl and a shout.

Jem sized up the skinny youth in the overalls who was trying to make his dog bark at her. He wore a white YPD cap. The yellow bars on the pocket showed he was full officer, not a 'Special' or 'Krew'. Rudi, his freakishly large Alsatian dog, ignored Nick's pleas for an aggressive snarl and sat quiet as a library mouse. Much to Nick's annoyance, Rudi loved to follow his own leads and only did what his handler said for one third of the time, at the last count.

'No need to read me my rights. These are my air tanks,' said Jem politely. 'And what's a Youth Police Department officer doing on an Adult Police station boat?' This was exactly what Jem's school

24

reports had meant when they talked about her 'lack of respect for authority figures.'

'The police forces are working together during The Emergency,' said the YPD.

'The Emergency? What's that? Otters in the pipes again is it?' asked Jem. 'Or that man-eating carp thing?'

'Drop those air tanks,' ordered the YPD, whose own report had said he needed to work on getting the right amount of chill in his voice when ordering people around.

'Wouldn't it be better if I put them away safely, in the air store?' Jem asked rather too nicely. 'Where all the good little tanks go to sleep at night.'

Nick was reaching into one of his many pockets for his book of penalty fine tickets, when the radio on his belt crackled. Rudi wagged his tail excitedly and snapped at the voice coming from the handset.

'Down Rudi!' yelled Nick, snatching the handset away from the dog's jaws. He didn't need to wind, it was charged and ready.

'Bravo Romeo Alpha Tango receiving,' said Nick.

Jem smiled. The call sign B.R.A.T just about summed this YPD up. No doubt he was too dim to get the 'Dults joke.

'Morning Nick,' said the voice of the operator. It was Sergeant. 'What've you got for us? Unauthorized swans on the water cannon?'

'Negative,' sighed Nick. He'd got the highest test score at Hendon Marsh where he'd done his training. After the results had been published, the rest of his class began to treat him like some kind of nut and started to whisper behind his back. Nick made a mental note of when they were laughing at him.

'Never interrupt your enemy when he is making a mistake,' as his hero Napoleon Bonaparte had put it.

CONTROL, I HAVE DETAINED A U.A.P. IN THE STORAGE AREA.

A U.A. WHAT?

For Nick, police jargon was kind of membership card – that kept outsiders apart from members of the club. Nick often spoke using letters instead of words. Sometimes he'd get through an entire sentence without using any nouns.

'A U.A.P., control,' said Nick slowly, 'An Unauthorized Person.'

'Give me a description, love,' said Sergeant.

'10 year-old female. Height about five-foot four. Blonde hair. Dressed in black with a green hat and sunglasses, police issue by the look of them. Possibly stolen.'

'They're mine. They were a present from my dad,' protested Jem, smarting from the officer's incorrect guess at her age.

'Shall I bring her in?' asked Nick, ignoring the pouting girl.

'Ask her to identify herself,' sniggered Sergeant.

'Name?' demanded Nick.

'A little 'please' wouldn't cost you anything,' said Jem.

'Name, please?' snapped Nick. Just then, Rudi made another grab for the radio, nipping his handler's gloved hand.

Nick shouted at the dog to 'CEASE', using another of the commands he'd been trying to teach the brute.

When that didn't work, he wrestled the radio from Rudi's jaws, getting his leather gloves all covered in slobber.

'Bravo Romeo Alpha Tango, be advised that your U.A.P is cleared to enter this area. Her name is Jemima Mallard.'

'Chief Inspector Mallard's daughter?'

'Yes. In the new spirit of police force co-operation you might want to go easy on her. She's had a tough week.'

'Copy that,' grunted Nick.

'You could show her round or something?' asked Sergeant.

'Could you really?' asked Jem eagerly.

Nick hesitated. He'd been assigned to work with the adult police, so the last thing he wanted was to offend a Chief Inspector.

'Well, I guess I could give you a quick tour,' offered Nick.

'Later!' smiled Jem. She slammed one of her air tanks into the storage rack and stomped off with the other, leaving the door open. Policeboy could wind it closed.

Suddenly, she was hit by 8 stone of Alsatian. Rudi had snatched Nick's radio and he sent Jem flying as he made his getaway. Her legs scrambled at nothing. Then, there was an inevitable splash.

Caught by the current, the air tank bobbed off downstream. Before Jem could swim after it, Nick ordered her to stay put. Then he leapt into a wooden rowing boat that was tied up to the jetty. As she trod the freezing water, Jem had to admit that Policeboy really knew his way around boats. He probably practiced emergency situations in his room or something.

Rudi barked excitedly as Nick maneuvered the boat towards Jem and held out an oar. When she'd reached the side, he hauled her up and slapped her on the deck like a trawlerman landing a haddock.

'Get my air!' screamed Jem again, pointing at the green tank that was rapidly disappearing downstream.

'Stay calm,' said Nick, heaving on the oars and bringing the boat around. Rudi gave a mournful howl as watched his handler row off.

Barking furiously, Rudi paddled after his disappearing master. Trying to swim and howl at the same time was difficult for the dog and he spluttered a whimper. Nick brought the boat around.

'What about my air!' demanded Jem in a rage. Nick's mind was already made up. His training told him not to act without thinking. The air tank was almost out of view now, floating towards the restricted zone. If he'd been on his own, he'd row hard and get it. But he had a passenger aboard. What if she fell out or something? Despite its size, the dog wasn't the strongest swimmer and couldn't climb a ladder on his own. Rudi wasn't exactly a 'valuable piece of police equipment', but nevertheless, Nick had a soft spot for the beast.

Nick said he'd put in a call to the next YPD station, down river. Jem gave the YPD another look that would boil a potato. Before she could find the right words, Rudi started barking again. He liked to follow his own leads. Now he'd cornered a suspect under the jetty: a small duck. It was tangled in a piece of netting, held fast to a wooden plank. Nick guided the boat in, bringing it alongside the rope ladder before turning to deal with Rudi's suspect. He cut away at the netting with the smallest blade on his penknife. The knife had been a graduation present from his instructors at the YPD's training centre at Hendon Marsh. Not everyone got on that well with their instructors at H.M! His prized possession had 17 blades. The young YPD had made a point of using each and every one in the course of his police duties. Untangling the duck was impossible on a moving boat so he cut away a large section of the net. It was a wonder that it had been able to swim, dragging that great tangle behind it.

Nick steadied the boat. He was balanced with the ladder in one hand and the struggling duck in the other. Reluctantly, he decided to ask the girl for help.

Jem sprang past the YPD and hauled herself up the ladder. In the air store, she grabbed her wetsuit and the last bottle of her 'birthday' air and stalked off along the jetty. At the end of a row of police launches was an old wooden 'Aquarama', with a YPD logo on it. 'Must be Policeboy's,' thought Jem.

The *Aqua* had an outboard motor – the type that you started by pulling on a cord. She gave the fuel tank a little swill and found it was about half full. There was no lock. Surely the YPD hadn't forgotten? Perhaps he thought no one would dare?

If you were planning to steal a police boat, it would make sense to slip the moorings, drift away downstream and get out of earshot of the guard dogs before starting your engine. Jem didn't give it much thought. If that idiot Policeboy wouldn't row out and get her birthday air, she'd 'borrow' his boat and get it for herself. She pulled the starter cord but the engine spluttered and died.

She gave it a second go, pulling on the cord harder this time. The YPD boats ran on bio fuel, made from fresh water beans or something. It was a devil to ignite, and it stank something rotten.

On the third pull the engine started with a rumble. She looked at the little 'rolling dice' that she'd stencilled onto her remaining air tank. The design showed three black and white dice in mid throw. Once the dice were cast, there was no going back. Pushing the throttle forward, the engine began to race. With a surge, the old boat leapt forward and slammed into to the jetty. A grinding crunch followed. Like a fool she'd put the motor into reverse! Sizable waves set the row of APD launches bobbing and bashing into each other. 'Fill!' muttered Jem, pulling back on the throttle this time and making off from the scene of her first serious crime.

Father Thames

'THAT'S BETTER, LITTLE FEATHER,' SAID SERGEANT, GENTLY STROKING THE DUCK'S WING. She'd set it down in a cardboard box. A sticker on the side of the box said: 'EVIDENCE – DO NOT DESTROY.'

'You'd better not touch it, it's a wild animal,' cautioned Nick.

'Don't you listen to him ducky,' cooed Sergeant, giving the little duck another stroke. It didn't seem to mind.

'It could carry diseases,' added Nick.

Sergeant gave him a dark look. At last, the tangle of netting wrapped around its foot gave way to the scissors blade of Nick's penknife.

'What've you got there ducky?' asked Sergeant.

Nick had found something in the tangled netting. It was small, about the size of an old ID card. But is was made out of a strange silver coated paper. Neither of the officers had seen anything like it before. On the front of the card was a black and white sketch of a rich man. He was wearing a top hat and leaning over the side of a riverboat. He held his nose as he offered something to a dark creature that was climbing out of the filthy water. The thing looked like some kind of sea monster with a human body. Its tangled beard was slimy with centuries of mud and rubbish. In its clawed hand, it clasped a devilish fork.

The top of the card bore an inscription in old-fashioned type:

Father Thames

'Father Thames, an ancient figure, a folk legend,' said Sergeant.

'Did he live in the river?' asked Nick.

'He was the river. He symbolized it. You know, like the Grim Reaper meant 'death' or Ronald McDonald stood for health food.'

'Right,' said Nick, not really knowing what she meant by this.

'Why's he all covered in muck?' asked Nick, noticing the black flies buzzing around the creature's hair.

'No idea,' said Sergeant, staring at the card for a moment. 'Do you mind if I hang on to that for a bit?' Sergeant placed the card on her desk and turned her attention to the duck.

She was about to search for the remainder of her sandwiches when the meeting room door swung open and C.I. Mallard entered. He took in the scene with a weary eye, wondering why his desk officer and the YPD liason were messing around with a duck.

Nick didn't laugh. He'd been ordered not to do or say anything that might damage relations between the adult police and the YPD. 'File it for me please Sergeant, in the river,' said the Chief Inspector, wearily.

'There's been another incident sir. Three miles down river, by a sink estate in Dock Lands.'

'That'll set tongues wagging,' said Mallard.

'They're wagging already sir. There's talk of water monsters. One of the bargers reckons he's seen one.' Mallard shook his head and smiled, stroking his moustache.

'Is he a reliable witness?' asked Nick.

'A reliable old soak, sir,' said Sergeant. Mallard smiled.

'Probably been at the bio fuel since sun up,' she added.

'Are the YPD across this?' asked Mallard.

Nick nodded. 'The incident has been reported. It'll be investigated in due course.'

'And sir – I thought you might like to see this,' said Sergeant holding up the card. The big man spun neatly on his heel.

35

Dead Slow

JEM POINTED THE NOSE OF THE AQUA AT THE HORIZON. A couple of kids in a pedalo stopped pedaling and began to wave. An old barger in a black hat shouted, shaking his tattooed fist. Jem couldn't understand why he was so furious. Then she spotted the little model ship that he'd just released into the current. It was full of burning offerings for the river gods. The bargers were still sailing their little boats out in hope, waiting for their 'great cargo' to come in. A skiff was blocking her course. Jem span the wheel and the *Aqua* obeyed.

At one stage, Jem had been impressed by the Washers cult. They believed that everything you wished for got washed away by a Flood Goddess – which Jem thought was a plus point. To be on the safe side, they spent all day wishing for nothing. Jem had found that part harder than it sounded.

'Slow down!' yelled an old wool seller in a flat-bottomed skiff.

Luckily Jem couldn't make out the rest of what he was saying over the roar of the *Aqua*'s engine. An old women shook her fist and pointed at a sign on the bank. It read: 'Dead Slow! Waves cause damage!' But Jem and the *Aqua* were gone in a puff of exhaust, ploughing on towards the floating market.

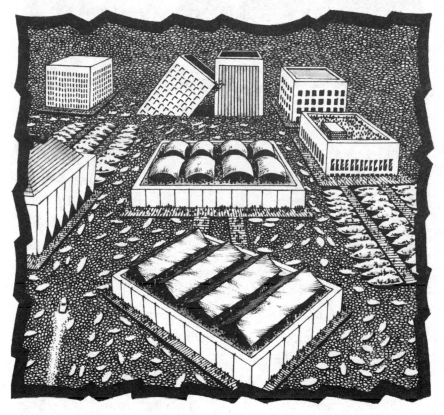

Jem wrestled with the wheel and narrowly avoided a bio tanker. Small craft scattered out of her way. The market traders stopped moaning about their rent increase and joined together to throw curses at Jem. The *Kong's Candles* boat was nearly capsized in the chaos, spilling its precious stock into the blue water.

'They're all gone!' cried a young candle seller, not guessing that her precious wax would float. Pretty soon she was fishing them out with a net borrowed from the tackle boat. A couple of traders decided that they'd had enough – and went off to moan at the management – who had the only fast boat on the market.

CALL NIPPER SECURITY!

Jem didn't notice the chaos she'd caused, any more than a wave notices the weeds. Steering a fast boat into the sun was a rare buzz. Nose into the waves, the sunlight dancing on the ripples, Jem thought that the river looked like the skin of a giant animal. As she skidded through the reflections, she thought about it but couldn't get the picture to form into words. The closest she'd got was in a dream where she'd discovered that the waves were the scales of a great blue serpent that wound its way across the back of the islands. Everything you could see was moving to tide and time – and Jem was a part of it all. She scanned the horizon for any glint of fluorescent green that might give away the location of the lost air tank. If she wanted to recover it, she'd have to act fast.

All the time she'd been escaping from Policeboy, her precious air tank had been drifting down stream. Eventually it would end up at the ocean, if it made it past the Thames Barrier Reef. The current itself came down the river in a rip that would carry a floating object at 8 miles an hour – and then there was the wind to think about. Making up for the lost time meant cruising a lot faster than she'd like. She told herself that she'd be OK so long as she stuck to the main channel where the water was a satisfying deep blue. Lighter water meant shallows – so Jem steered away from the light water. And then, a rare treat. Two young bottle-nosed dolphins were racing her boat – twisting out of the water as they vied for the lead. As soon as one of them got in front, it gave up the lead and dropped back level with the other, ready to race again. Jem guessed that the book she'd been reading would probably find something deep about this. But she couldn't be bothered to put any energy into that line of thought.

Jem cut the throttle. There was a shout and the unmistakable sound of an outboard motor. The market security boat put-putted round the bend. Swimming with dolphins was the last thing on their minds, they always kept a spare harpoon in the boat.

Jem gunned the throttle again and the old boat charged forward, its nose rearing up. Policeboy would swoon if he'd heard his engine screaming like this. He probably never took it past four thousand revs. Now the *Aqua*'s nose was rearing so high out of the water that Jem nearly lost it. She glanced behind her and couldn't see the market security boat – eventually she spotted a tiny dot in the far distance.

Swinging the *Aqua* left and sticking to the deepest channel, Jem muscled the boat through bend after bend. She was loving this! Till she spotted the tell-tale wasp stripe of YPD tape that marked the edge of a restricted area. There were the usual notices saying that anything floating out of the area needed to be handed in to the police forces. Then she felt it.

There was a sickening crack and the *Aqua* lurched to a halt. 'A dead man,' thought Jem. There was no shortage of tales about river creatures – made up to frighten curious children into behaving themselves. Jem wasn't afraid of the Old River Man or the Wounded Sirens. But her worst fear was 'dead men' – submerged trees that lurked beneath the water's surface. Hitting one at speed could hole your boat and break your neck. Worse still were 'electrics' – ancient steel towers that could gut your boat and suck you down to the tangled world below.

Jem scanned the horizon. It was a lonely bend in the river. The only thing in sight were the tips of a couple of sunken tower blocks.

Then she spotted water, where it shouldn't be, a thin puddle around her feet. Unusually for the Thames, the water had a brown tinge to it. Jem drew a line on the base of the seat. It seemed a shame to spoil pale green leather with red crayon – but it was her or the upholstery! She looked at the puddle for what seemed like an age. Was water getting in? Or was it just spray from the crash? Examining the *Aqua*'s side, she found a long scratch along the prow. The timber was all chewed up but the marks disappeared half way down the side. Had the *Aqua* been holed below the water? Jem stared at the level of the puddle as it crept slowly over her crayon mark. Jem slipped skillfully over the side. The water felt as cold as ever, even through a triple skinned suit. It was a brownish-yellow colour. This was going to be like diving in Miso soup. Jem attached a line to the side of the boat and struggled with her torch. Nothing! She'd forgotten to wind it. Hanging onto the side with one arm, she fiddled with the winding mechanism. A sudden swell made her lose her footing and she dropped the torch. 'Fill!' she winced. Breathing out, she plunged after it and kicked for the bottom, her eyes fixed on the disappearing glow.

With a couple of kicks she thought she'd almost caught it. But distances are hard to estimate underwater. Suddenly, she felt a sensation on her hands. It was like swimming through a shoal of tiny fish or weeds. By the time she'd grabbed the torch, she'd got no idea of how far away the boat was. Once again Jem found herself winding power into the torch, wasting precious air. Dad was right, she just wouldn't stop, think, observe. With one quick flick, the river lit up around her and Jem gasped.

At first she thought she'd strayed into some great underwater forest, for she was floating in the middle of an enormous curtain of falling leaves. Or were they flowers? They were white, red, yellow, all different colours against the brown water. Jem wiped frantically at her face. Something had wrapped itself around her mask. Then everything went dark.

Rudi

Nick struggled up the ladder in a sulk, clutching the evidence box containing the duck. He didn't need a pet. He'd already got Rudi. Everyone had warned him that a reject police dog would be trouble, but Nick wasn't bothered. Rudi was the closest thing to an old-school attack dog you could get, although he'd proved impossible to train. Nick had named Rudi after a famous mayor of Old New York who invented 'intolerant' policing. The instructors said that was the start, when the police took back control from the underlife.

Nick had never been past the Isle of Frogs but sometimes he dreamed about being a cop in Old New York. He even wore his NYPD cap on duty sometimes – as the letters were nearly the same as YPD and the N could stand for Nick. It worked, sort of. Besides, the YPD had run out of bigger cap sizes. Nick was praying this didn't get out. You can guess what the 'Dult's would have to say about swell-headed cop kids. And there was no way he could keep a duck named after an ADP Chief Inspector in his cabin. The station would talk. 'C.I. Mallard' had two choices: it was back to the wild, or a long slow sleep in a roasting tin.

Rudi stared blankly at the space where the *Aqua* had been, turned his great head and gave a puzzled bark. Nick shook his head and cursed under his breath. What was the river coming to? Were the underlife getting so cocky that they'd dare to steal a boat when it was tied to a police barge? This would not stand!

Whilst a part of him was rightly angry about the crime, in his heart, he knew the truth. Nick had deliberately left his boat unlocked – hoping that someone would steal it. He was well prepared for this situation. He hoped with all his heart that it was kids. If the boat thief was an adult, the 'Dult cops would get the credit. But if it was kids, it was a YPD case, so the collar would be all his. Nick had the fourth best arrest record in the division and was gunning for third place – held by a sad kid called Nailor who liked to call himself 'The Hammer'. He pulled a small black box out of his pocket and flicked its single unmarked switch to the 'on' position. Naturally, the tracker was wound up and ready to go. It let out a sequence of beeps which could lead him to the *Aqua*. Nick allowed himself a smile as he thought about how clever this system was. It would work for as long as the battery in the transmitter held. Luckily, Nick loved winding things up. He got up early and did all his winding every morning, in the same strict order. It had at least a few hours life in it. Now all he needed was a pursuit craft. But looking down the rank, there were only 'Dult boats available.

Rudi wagged his tail but when he realised he was tied up, he let out a pitiful howl. 'No chance,' laughed Nick, hittting starter button. 'Remember what happened the last time I took you on a ski?'

Mask

JEM RUBBED AT HER MASK. The strange substance came apart in her fingers, dissolving into mush. A couple of kicks took her clear of the cloud, whatever it was. A cold beam lit the water far below her. Jem had never seen a light so bright. She began to kick towards it. When the murk cleared, she saw a shape.

As quick as it had appeared, the light and the figure were suddenly gone. In the darkness, it felt instantly colder. She thought about air. How long had she been down now? She'd lost track.

Jem knew that if you spotted an unknown shape at this depth, you weren't supposed to float right up to it and say 'Hi!', but curiosity got the better of her. With a couple of neat kicks she set off towards where she thought she'd seen the movement. Allowing herself to rise a little bit, she was hoping to place herself on a level above whatever was down there. Diving was a little bit like flying in that respect. She'd read somewhere that the fighter pilots of old would rise to the heavens, get the sun at their backs and then swoop down upon their unsuspecting targets.

She was breathing calmly now. For a long while there was nothing but murk and she was about to head for the surface when there it was again: a strange light, snaking across the water to her left. Through the gloom she made out a blurred shape that made her shiver. Something about twice the size of a tall man was walking along the riverbed.

Mud exploded from the thing's mouth, clouding the clear water. Through the swirling murk, Jem caught sight of a single orange eye.

This was a first for Jem. But the Thames was an old river, deep enough to hide all manner of secrets.

Jem's last school report had said that 'Jemima is a girl who doesn't know when to be sensible.' Right now, she was feeling sensible. Whatever perils awaited (including a dark night in a holed boat) must be better than a face-off with whatever was eating its way through the riverbed. She adjusted her belt and began to swim upwards, pleased with her good sense. Even her dad would approve. Rising serenely, she remembered to check the gauge on her air tank.

ALMOST EMPTY!

Jem took a hurried gulp but found she was sucking on nothing. Was the gauge faulty? She flicked to the reserve tank - that would give her another 6 minutes at most. Jem knew she couldn't risk going up too fast. Every diving book that she'd read warned of what 'the bends' could do. If divers surfaced too quickly, tiny bubbles of gas in their blood started to break out of their veins. The pain was supposed to be beyond words, but the books all had a go at describing it. Words like 'bulging' usually came into it. Hanging for a moment, Jem found herself still 10 metres down.

She was too deep to kick for the surface. She needed to wait for the deadly gas to leave her bloodstream. As the seconds passed, Jem felt the water get colder. She'd read somewhere that you lost a degree of temperature for every five metres of depth. Or had she made that up to win an argument with her dad? Jem began to panic. Only three minutes of air left. Out of time! Then she dived in a crazy direction: down.

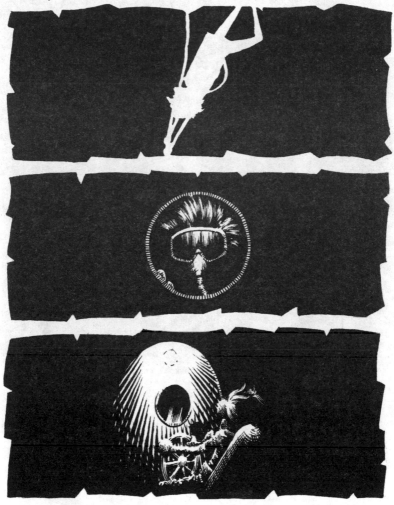

Green light was streaming out of the porthole, into the water around her. But the craft – whatever it was, was empty. 'Let there be air in there – please!' thought Jem.

She fumbled around the body of the craft for anything that looked like a hatch. The outside of the craft was smooth, bathed in that cold green light.

'Fool!' She screamed at herself as she peered upwards through the murk. Bends or no bends, it was time to kick for the surface.

Jem had never been so pleased to see a YPD diver before! He took the regulator from his mouth and handed it to her. The air mixture tasted sweet. As they rose slowly to the surface, Jem had only one thing on her mind. 'Rescued by Policeboy! The shame of it!' She was glad that she didn't have a permanent school right now, that rumours couldn't get about. It would probably be all around the station boat canteen though.

Jem had to admire the way that Nick guided her up to the surface. He knew what he was doing, bringing them up right next to the ladder at the bow of the *Aqua* where he'd tied his ski. She tried to play it low key as she removed her mask.

Policeboy did likewise. He was probably loving this! Jem noticed the white pressure marks around his eyes where his face mask had been digging in.

'But you can't arrest me! I was only borrowing your boat!'

'You have no rights, so remain silent,' said Nick coldly.

'I thought you wouldn't mind,' protested Jem.

Jem spent the next ten minutes thinking up interesting ways to kill him.

The Keep and The Tower

'HERE'S WHERE YOU GET OFF,' SAID NICK AS HE EXPERTLY MANEUVERED THE JET SKI UP TO THE SIDE OF THE KEEP. Jem had never been this close to a YPD holding cell before, and she didn't like the look of it. It was a small wooden capsule – little bigger than a coffin, sticking up from the river like a thin rocket on a stick.

Clinging to Nick as they skied over the swells, Jem had wondered where the YPD officer was taking her. For a second she dreamed that he might let her off with a caution. Not Nick. He was as low on compassion as he was on regular passion. She'd begged him to put a call in to her father, but he'd refused. This was a YPD matter – there was no need to get the 'Dult police involved.

Once he'd gone, Jem remembered Nick's caution. 'The keep will start to sink if you try to escape!'

Resting her hand on the wall Jem found it clammy to the touch. The air was musty.

She had a thought: how many of the so called 'dead men' that riddled the river's channels were actually YPD keeps? Only the YPD knew their exact positions. And when they weren't being used, they waited silently below the water until they were needed. Jem peered out at the lonely water. The river was wide here, so wide that she couldn't make out the opposite bank. It was empty save for a lone duck drifting in her direction. Jem recalled Nick's warning and imagined sinking in this cage. It was nothing short of evil to put the fear into her with thoughts like that. Surely he couldn't be serious about it sinking with her inside? In a rage, she lashed out:

As water poured into the Keep, Jem battered the door with kicks till it finally gave up and came off its hinges. She pushed herself out and trod water, gasping at the cold. At first she thought about swimming down river and aiming for the Island. Then she had an idea. The Keep behind her was not completely under water. She swam back and clambered onto the roof to get a better vantage point.

As Jem stood on the roof of the flooded Keep, she noticed the number 8224 etched into the woodwork below her. Did the YPD have eight thousand of these things on the river? Scanning the horizon, she saw nothing within swimming distance. Here the Thames was wide, like a great lake. Looking down, she found herself face-to-face with the only thing on the river, a small white duck. Then she noticed something extraordinary. Around the duck's neck was a waterproof envelope – no bigger than a playing card. Wary of the duck's beak, Jem unhooked the envelope and removed the contents.

Jem examined the shiny card. It was almost entirely golden in colour. Something drew her attention from it for a moment and she looked up. A fog was rising as a couple of swans flew over. When Jem turned her attention to the card again she noticed that a tiny patch of the gold colour appeared to have rubbed off, revealing a different colour beneath. Before she could give it any more thought, Jem was shaken by the blast of a klaxon. Instinctively, she slipped the card into the inside pocket of her wetsuit.

The galley loomed large through the swirling fog, and Jem wondered how they'd found out about her breakout. Escape wasn't an option. There was nowhere in the open water she could reach before the galley picked her up. Jem threw bitter curses at the approaching ship, and saved a few for her own bad fortune. Now she could add 'escaping from a YPD facility' to her lengthening charge sheet. Jem saw the tall mast, and below it, the deck where the prisoners crouched, sweating at the oars. The galley had sails of course, but it was typical of the YPD to set their prisoners to work, even before they arrived in prison. This galley wasn't running on 'perp' power – it was empty save for a boy, whistling like a dolphin as he sweated at the oars.

A few minutes later, Jem found herself sitting next to the kid, strapped in tight. As she glared at the guard in his white 'Krew' uniform, she wondered if her fellow prisoner was right in the head. He must have been no more than ten years old, although big with it. Around his waist he was wearing a pink rubber ring and rowing as if his life depended on it. His name was Saul.

Trust the YPD to invent a tagging device that made you look like an idiot! The old bracelets they used to use were too cool. Jem stopped pretending to row and craned her neck to take in her surroundings. There was no sign of guards so she fumbled in her pocket and took out the card.

'Get rowing. Why have you stopped?' asked Saul.

'Unlike you, I've got no desire to help them kidnap me,' sneered Jem.

'There's no dinner, unless you row,' explained Saul.

'Suits me,' shrugged Jem.

Saul slowed his pace and fixed Jem with a purposeful stare.

'No dinner means no dinner for either of us,' explained Saul impatiently. 'I'm starved, so would you get off your high horse and put that scratcher away before the Krew see it?'

Jem considered her options for a moment, and then got rowing.

Time flowed like bio from a holed drum. Every half an hour one of the Krew came down to check on the prisoners. There wasn't much to do except row. Jem began to feel the tiredness building in her shoulders.

'Did you find the scratcher by one of them gurges?' asked Saul, unexpectedly.

'What?' mumbled Jem. She was normally cool with barger slang but didn't have a clue what the boy was on about.

'Your scratcher,' repeated Saul, pointing at the card. 'Did you find it by a gurge?'

'Oh – yeah,' said Jem, hoping to shut him up.

'Have you scratched it off yet? Let me see.' Jem looked nervously at the ladder.

'Don't worry about the Krew – they're on a rota. Won't be back for another 15 minutes.'

Slowly, Jem took the card from her pocket again and looked at Saul. Without asking, he took it from her hand.

'Where are we being taken?' asked Jem.

Saul stopped rowing, lent forwards and prised open a slat. Jem stood up and peeped through the hole. Out of the mist, two great spikes rose out of the river. A walkway joined the two towers, forming a giant letter 'H' that loomed out of the river like fangs. It had been someone's idea of a laugh to base the design on the old Tower Bridge. Someone else had got hold of some red paint and decorated the tips of the 'teeth' in red for good measure.

'It's the YPD's largest prison hulk, so you'll be in bad company,' said Saul.

A cold sensation seeped through Jem's body – like water through a holed boot. As she pulled out the card from her pocket, Saul caught her eye then grabbed her hand.

'I'll look after that for you. You'll be searched before you go in.'

'No thanks,' said Jem. But before she could protest, she heard the thud of boots on the ladder. As the guards arrived, Saul made the card disappear under his palm.

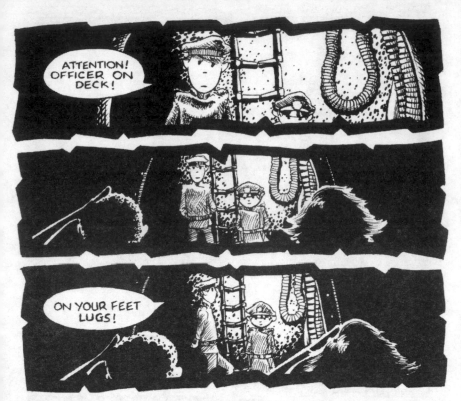

Neither of the guards were more than ten years old. Jem wondered how their perfect eyes hadn't spotted Saul stuffing the card into his shoe.

Jem felt slightly sick as she followed Saul up the series of ladders that lead to the deck. When the two offenders showed their faces on deck – they were greeted by a distant glow. Hundreds of tiny lights danced on the walkway between the two great towers.

They were drawing closer to the tower now, and Jem could make out tiny figures on the gantry, their arms outstretched and waving. As they drew near, the wind suddenly gusted into their faces, carrying with it a great shriek – high in pitch – the sound of young voices wailing.

'Whatever happened to tying a yellow ribbon round the Old Marsh Oak?' asked Jem. She was starting to think that she was lucky to have someone like Saul around. An old hand, who if he wasn't going to actually show her the ropes, would at least stop her from tripping over them. The Krewman fiddled with the radio and then began to wind it. The first of two small transport boats, sent from the prison, was approaching the galley. Its skipper tied onto the side of the galley.

'Thanks,' said Jem trying to hide her disappointment at losing both Saul and her mysterious card.

'Boat B,' muttered the smaller of the Krewmen.

'Do I, er, follow him then?' asked Jem.

The Krewman looked at his mate and raised an eyebrow.

'I'd knight that remark, if were you, froggy!' spat the other, rubbing his hand along the long stick at his belt.

'Knight it?'

'You have to call them 'Sir' whenever you speak to them,' yelled Saul from the ladder. 'She's new Sir, but she'll pick it up quick,' he added.

The Krewman glared at Jem as if she was a piece of scum he'd just discovered on his new surf suit.

'Sorry, I mean do I follow him now, please Sir?' asked Jem politely, starting to release what kind of trouble she was in.

The first Krewman sniggered at her grovelling tone.

'Stop blabbing,' he ordered.

'It's Boys to A Tower, Girls to B Tower, right Sir?' called Saul.

'Move!' yapped the Krewman, waving Saul away like a bad smell from the bilges.

Saul stepped into the little boat where the skipper cuffed him to the side. He wasn't allowed to speak – but his eyes said goodbye as he hauled through the chop. Now Jem was alone at the rail of the galley. With her father being an Inspector in the adult police, Jem had adopted a grown up view of the 'police kids' – the YPD and their little Krew helpers. Any force full of bossy seven-year-olds prancing around in white uniforms is hard to take that seriously. But now who knew what the brats had planned for her. There was nothing to do but wait for her prison ride. Then another boat pulled up through the mist and swept alongside.

'I've got a warrant for one of your prisoners,' it crackled. 'Call headquarters if you don't believe me, love.' Jem couldn't believe her luck. It was Sergeant.

'I'm throwing a line,' crackled the loud hailer.

The rope was expertly coiled and pitched. It landed on the deck of the galley just three steps away from the smaller Krewman. Jem was impressed – she had only seen Sergeant sailing a desk before.

After a minute of discussions that Jem couldn't make out, the smaller Krewman began to fiddle with the radio, cursing and then winding it up in a fury. Jem's eyes were on the rope. She gawped at the thin blue line – as if that rope might haul her back to her own world and connect her with her family again. Then the Kaptain emerged from his cabin and strolled towards the rope. He picked it up, and smirking, flung it back into the grey water.

As the current edged the two boats towards each other, Jem noticed Sergeant's expression. Not aggressive, not challenging – but cold, like half-submerged rock. A womanly, middle-aged rock. Calmly, Sergeant hauled the discarded rope back in. Her eyes never left the officer in charge as she hauled back the rope. The rope found its own way into a neat figure of eight coil. Jem, who was more familiar with Sergeant's biscuit eating skills, was impressed at this new side to the officer.

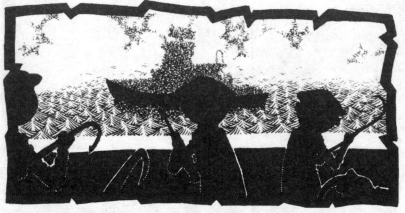

Three Krew members had joined The Kaptain on deck and were ready with boat hooks poised to fend off Sergeant's launch if she attempted to force her way on board. Relations between the two forces were rocky at best.

You coud always expect the YPD to behave like kids, and her dad's lot were no better. But to attempt a rescue in YPD waters could be the cause of a major incident. Jem couldn't imagine what Sergeant was going to try next.

But Sergeant didn't have to do anything, for the current had put her boat in between the little prison transport craft and the YPD galley.

If the kiddy cops wanted to take Jem in, they'd have to change course. Jem thought she saw a tiny flicker of a smile come over Sergeant's face, but it was gone in an instant.

The Krew began to curse and jeer insults at the 'Dults. At a command from the Kaptain, the galley turned in a slow arc, bringing itself in close to the Tower. It was no easy task. The little transport boat had checked its speed to a dead slow as the skipper tried to second guess the wind and currents.

It was then cat and mouse, with the three boats changing tack in order to gain advantage. Slowly, ever so slowly, the galley got the upper hand. Two Krew members escorted Jem to the other side of the boat and made ready with a ladder. Without a word from the white uniforms, her hands were untied. They'd be needed for the treacherous climb. As they finally got in close, Jem spotted the floating pontoons that held up the great towers. They were fixed to the cruel rocks by steel pins.

Viscous-looking wire defended each tower - but it was facing inwards to prevent escape. As Jem made ready for the slippery climb down the ladder, she noticed a shadow in the clear blue water below her. The shadow began to grow and take shape, clusters of tiny bubbles clinging to it as it rose. When Jem recognised the shape, she could hardly register what was happening. Surely, the Krew would see it too? With a splutter of foam, the dark object emerged from the waves.

A hatch at the top of the little craft opened – and the head of a large Alsatian dog poked out. The dog was joined by grey-haired man sporting with the sort of mustache that would look good on a circus strongman.

Jem didn't need to be asked twice. In an instant, she launched herself off the galley and splashed into the waves at the base of the ladder.

The Krewman was about to follow Jem into the waves – but a savage growl from Rudi stopped him in his tracks. The dog's lips quivered as he bared his teeth. Rudi may have been a reject police dog, but thanks to Nick's regular brushing, he had the whitest teeth in the YPD in his long jaws. The Krewman had second thoughts, scrambled for a boat hook and began to prod it at the snarling dog. Rudi wagged his tail as he snapped at the boat hook. He was enjoying this game! He made a few ill-timed lunges at the hook, barking in between snaps for good measure. As the Krew yelled threats and protests, their Kaptain pushed forwards towards the ladder.

'Assisting a prisoner to escape is against the law,' he called. 'You should know that at your age. And while you're in our waters, you'd better stay legal.'

Mallard fixed the youth with a glare.

'Do know what your 'prisoner' was up to, when you pulled her? She was diving in a Black Hole. That makes it my business.'

'She's for The Tower,' called the YPD. 'And there'll be worse for you, unless you hand her back.'

'Then please proceed, Kaptain,' said Mallard. The galley had water cannon, but no weaponry aboard that could damage Mallard's mini sub. It was a museum piece but its steel hull was three inches thick.

'Thanks dad,' said Jem, making herself as small as possible as her father battened down the hatch.

'Don't thank me yet love,' said Mallard, puffing slightly. 'And give the hell hound a mint or something? Its breath reeks like a midden.'

As the blue Thames swallowed the sub and the Kaptain of Galley 39 made his report, a white duck emerged from its hiding

68

place under the base of the Tower. Tipping its head to one side, it span around in circles in the sub's wake.

Jem tugged on Rudi's collar and tried to pull his head away from her dad's face as she waited for a telling off. She knew she'd be 'moored' for weeks, so she decided she'd try talking this time.

Talking things through wasn't really one of her dad's strong points either. The waters ahead were clear but it was a challenge to pilot the tiny sub through the notorious Mayfair Swamp by sight alone. The sub's batteries were limited, and Mallard didn't want to waste power on sonar unless it was strictly necessary.

Jem tried again. 'Dad. Where are we going now?'

'Home,' came the answer.

'We don't have a home. It got sunk, remember?'

'Ah!' said Mallard – as if he'd actually forgotten that *The Strangetown* had been sunk. Jem didn't see much of her dad. And when she saw him, she didn't understand him much of the time. All of his stuff had gone down with their boat too: medals and memories, all on the riverbed. But this traumatic event appeared to have slipped his mind. Jem wondered what he spent his waking hours thinking about?

'Well, it's back to the station then, to scale the north face of your paperwork,' shrugged the Chief Inspector.

'Er, thanks dad,' said Jem.

'I told you not to thank me yet love. You know I can't help you till you're grown up.'

Jem thought about what a heap of fill it was being a kid.

She patted Rudi's head. 'What are you doing here boy? Where's your owner?'

'That dog's on his holidays,' grunted Mallard. 'His owner, sadly, is not.'

Room for a 'view

Mallard stopped outside a closed cell and told Jem to wait outside with Rudi. As her dad entered, Jem peeped into the room. Across the desk sat Nick, next to another YPD officer. Jem guessed that he was of higher rank than Nick, if the blue piping around his uniform was anything to go by. The kid's name was Haig. He looked really young – not more than 8 years old. His body was thin, almost weedy but his face still had that puffed up quality that you see on a plump toddler. Before her dad closed the door Jem caught his gaze, noticing his huge eyes. She found the combination of an old head on a young body a bit creepy.

It was a long wait before she was called in. She decided to make friends with Rudi by throwing sweets for the dog to catch in his mouth. She figured that this would annoy his owner – who'd probably have him on some special power diet or something.

At last, the door swung open and Sergeant beckoned her in.

Sergeant sighed. Without another word, Mallard walked out.

'I've got a question,' said Jem. 'How come you YPD can just lock up whoever you like, stick them in a hulk and leave them to rot. I'm amazed that your 'Bloody Tower' actually exists. It's backward, barbaric...' Jem looked towards the door as she finished the sentence, wishing that her dad hadn't left.

Haig sat calmly through her little outburst, smiling like a baby-faced crocodile. He didn't answer, as if he was waiting for Nick to reply on behalf of the YPD.

'If you hadn't stolen my boat you wouldn't be here now. Break the law or don't, it's your choice,' said Nick matter-of-factly. He was supposed to be playing 'nice cop' but he wasn't much good at it. His instructor at YPD training in Hendon Lock said that Nick needed to work harder at being interested in people. That said it all really.

'That's enough love,' advised Sergeant, whose report had said she was too interested in people. However, her advice was lost on Jem, who was getting nicely warmed up now. She glared at Nick as if she was about to strike him.

'We usually cuff our prisoners during interviews,' smirked Haig. 'We find it's the most sensible way.'

'Some kids sank my boat,' raged Jem. 'You did nothing. Then your reject cop dog knocked my air into the river and you stopped me from going after it. Where's the justice in that?'

'Is that Father Thames talking?' asked Nick.

'Father Thames?' replied Jem, rather unconvincingly.

Haig looked up from the paperwork. Suddenly, Jem was aware of his eyes fixed upon her. He concentrated his attention on her, channeling it like a torch beam. He'd been trained in certain methods for interviewing suspects. Sergeant sighed, she guessed that the boy was putting on this show for her and Nick. He'd signaled to all that his demonstration was about to begin.

It was as if only he and she existed. All others in the room were as important as the tables and chairs.

Jem almost bought it, for a moment. Then she smiled. She remembered Saul and all the others like him, locked up in the Tower. Haig had called Father Thames a terrorist. But if Father Thames was against the YPD, maybe he had a point?

'Actually Jem, your father was hoping you could throw some light on Father Thames – and then perhaps these officers could help you out by dropping the charges against you,' said Sergeant.

'That would depend,' said Haig.

'Your information would need to be something valuable, that would lead to arrests,' added Nick eagerly. He'd never had an informer before and was quite excited about the prospect.

'I've had a message, from them,' said Jem.

'Like this calling card, with the monster on it?' demanded Nick.

'Mine's much better than that one. It's a personal message, from Father Thames himself,' said Jem.

Haig threw his head back and began to scoff. 'You're an expert storyteller,' said Haig, reading from the paperwork in front of him. 'Your teacher says you have a 'remarkable imagination.'

'It's true,' insisted Jem.

'Go on, waste a little more police time,' hissed Haig.

'What does the message say?' asked Nick.

'I don't know what it says yet. You have to scratch it to reveal it.'

'That's fill,' said Haig, mocking her. 'You lie like a 'Dult.'

'Yeah? Can I go on a course, so I can learn to lie like you?'

The three officers watched in amazement as the thin layer of silver began to rub away. Slowly, a picture of two curved swords appeared. Next to the swords was written:

PRS NTR 2 RLS H20

'The one I've got is gold. That means it's from the Father himself,' called Jem.

Three minutes later they were back in the room with an offer. They'd drop all charges in return for Jem's full story and the other scratch card.

'She accepts,' said Sergeant immediately.

Jem nodded. Spinning a story would be easy, but what about her card? They wouldn't believe her if she told the truth about Saul hiding it in his shoe. And she didn't want to get Saul into any more trouble. She slipped her hand into her pocket and began to fumble.

'No!' she cried in despair, searching frantically at each pocket. 'Gone! It's gone!' she began to sob.

'Nice try,' said Haig. 'But I'm not going to let you make a fool of the YPD. It's back to The Tower for you. We'll find out everything we need to, in our own time.'

'Only kidding,' said Jem. 'You don't think I'd be stupid enough to keep it here, do you? But I've showed you how they work. How they pass their messages – that should be proof that I'm serious.'

'It's proof that you're up to your neck in untruths,' said Nick, rather pleased with his turn of phrase.

Haig remained silent, fixed on Jem.

'Your card has another message on it – like this one – that's right isn't it love?' asked Sergeant .

'Yes. Well, I don't know for sure, I haven't scratched it off yet,' said Jem honestly.

Haig nodded. She was telling the truth at last.

'Where is it?' demanded Nick.

'Somewhere safe,' said Jem. 'I can show you.'

'Well – I suppose you two had better go and get it,' said Haig. 'Bring it to me and we'll talk.'

'But your offer stands about dropping all charges?' asked Sergeant.

'My offer stands,' said Haig. 'The truth is important to me, as you'll learn.'

'I'll have it in writing, if you don't mind,' said Sergeant.

Outside the interview room, Mallard grabbed Jem by the hand.

Cold Metal

THE SMALL WHITE DUCK SEEMED TO BE DRIFTING EFFORTLESSLY, BUT IF YOU COULD ROLL UP THE RIVER LIKE A BLANKET AND PEEK UNDER THE GREY WAVES, YOU'D BE SURPRISED TO SEE HOW MUCH PADDLING WAS GOING ON. When the bird knew the time was right, it turned its head out of the wind and paddled up a smaller channel. The surface of the water here was smoother. A tangled ring of swamp oaks gave the spot some shelter. The wind, which was busy pushing its way to work down the old Thames, gave up at the mouth of this lagoon. Here the duck disappeared from view. It forced itself down on a deep dive, acting on some unknown instinct. Downwards it pushed, only leveling off when it came to a rocky shelf on the riverbed. Thinking about nothing more mysterious than its next meal, it began to snake its way into the metal pipe and was swallowed whole.

Two Swords

THE ROOM THAT HAD BEEN DARK WAS NOW LIT BY THE PULSE OF FLASHING NEON. The gas in the bulb burned wastefully, throwing light on a fat man with a goatee beard. The man flicked a pill upwards, caught it on his tongue tip and began to crunch it into a bitter mush. As usual, his stomach was killing him. It hurt when he ate. It hurt more when he didn't eat. It even hurt when he thought about food. It was a wonder that he only got through a packet of these pills a day. A neat brown haired woman entered the room, wrinkled her nose and gave a small disapproving cough. She always seemed to be looking whenever the fat man was carrying out one of the many bodily functions that are best performed without an audience.

THE STATS ARE IN: SEVENTY-FIVE THOUSAND LITRES. MAYBE MORE IF THE GAS GODS WILL IT.

THAT WON'T DO.

THATS ALL WE'LL GET OUT OF THE PIPE - UNLESS YOU WANT TO RISK ANOTHER ACCIDENT.

The Fatman spun off his chair and strutted to the other side of the room and hit a button on one of his remotes. An electric motor whirred and hydraulics lifted and swiveled the nesting chamber around in one easy action. The Fatman smiled as he always did whenever one of his gadgets performed its function exactly as programmed, which was about 72.5 percent of the time according to his computer. The idea of training ducks to nest underwater had come to him after he'd been watching a spy movie from the 1980's. Its portly secret agent hero had escaped from a pagoda by strapping a model duck onto his balding head.

The room erupted into a chaotic mess of flapping, pecking and quacking. With a graceful stoop, the Fatman grabbed a duck that had flapped up onto a tower of scientific measuring equipment. Cupping its body in his chubby hand, he began to stroke its head. When the duck relaxed, the Fatman pounced, pulling at its tail and emerging with a long white feather between his finger and thumb. Once this operation was over, the duck gave the Fatman a wounded look, pecked at its tail feathers and then settled down to its reward – a special mixture of low fat food. The Fatman pulled up a chair and stuck the end of the feather into an interface in the ancient rack of computing equipment. The old monitor woke from its slumbers and a video clip began to play. Shaky footage showed a miserable girl, stranded on the roof of a YPD Keep.

London Deep

NICK WAS LOSING PATIENCE. They'd been crossing and recrossing this area of river, wasting precious bio on a fruitless search. Inspector Mallard's girl was a 'fantasist' as her psyc file had put it. One look at the sample of her handwriting should have been enough to convince any shrink that she was a bit twisted.

The fuel gauge read a quarter to empty. Nick had already warned Jem that they'd need to head back before it kissed the red line on the dial. Whilst the girl was clearly a liar, there was nothing to gain from a confrontation with her. He'd better make it the fuel tank's fault.

bank with a jab of the oar. A shabby looking swan poked its neck out and hissed at Nick.

'Dumb bird' muttered the YPD.

'If you kept your dumb oar out of its nest, it might behave itself,' scoffed Jem. 'Isn't there a rule about bothering wildlife?'

'Time's up,' declared Nick, ever so slightly smug. But Jem didn't hear him. Her eye had been taken by something in the swans' nest – an uncomfortable jumble of sticks. In the middle of the nest was a multi-coloured tangle. Wires and strips of plastic lined the nest. 'We're close,' said Jem.

'Fraid your time's up,' repeated Nick matter-of-factly. He'd got the prow of the boat set for the centre of the channel and was just pulling back the throttle when he felt Jem's hand over his own, on the tiller. Before he could protest, Jem had aimed the boat at a small gap in the reeds where two twisted swamp oaks formed a natural arch.

The flat-bottomed boat skimmed over a mass of vegetation and broke through into the lagoon beyond. There was no tape announcing its presence, but Nick knew immediately that they were drifting towards an immense Black hole. The biggest he'd ever seen.

The two watched it slowly revolving, trying to read intentions in its ripples. The insects buzzed aimlessly around. Every now and again, the great whirl let out an occasional burst of bubbles, as if it wanted them to know that it was there. Like a volcano, a Black hole could go active at any time.

Nick timed the interval between the bubbles – they were coming about every two minutes.

At first glance, the surface almost looked divable. On closer inspection, there were patches of rough water and shifting ripples, evidence of strong currents in there.

'I didn't just chuck it in,' said Jem. 'But if you don't fancy the dive – that's fine, I'll recover it myself.' Nick watched as a small white duck floated towards the centre of the whirl, dipped its head in and disappeared. Nick did a quick risk assessment. He gazed at the water, as if trying to solve a puzzle. He counted for three minutes.

'That duck hasn't come back up,' he said.

'They're great divers – ducks!'

'Hmmm. There could be strong currents down there.'

'Thank you for pointing that out officer. What fine minds in the YPD! There could be strong currents in a Black hole. Don't you think I might be able to work that out myself, seeing as my home was swallowed by one!' Jem stopped chiding and smiled. She'd done her own 'assessment' of their situation, congratulating herself on her quick thinking. Either he lets me dive alone, and I'll disappear. Or he leaves me on the boat and dives alone – and I'll disappear. Either way – it's bye-bye Policeboy.

'You'd better let me dive,' said Jem soothingly. 'I'll be back in 5 minutes.' Then Nick did something uncharacteristic.

'Clip this on,' he said finally, throwing her a rope and harness.

'But I don't have a mask,' said Jem.

'We'll buddy breathe,' said Nick.

'But I can't! I mean – it might be risky, I've not had any training,' said Jem, trying to appeal to the YPD's love of rules and regulations. But Nick was ahead of her.

'It'll be no problem for a diver of your experience.'

Jem groaned aloud at the thought of sharing a mask covered in Nick's spit. Then she smiled a bit too enthusiastically.

Two handovers later, Jem felt something brush past her in the gloom. She fumbled for her torch, but couldn't get it working. Nick reached for his, which was fully wound. The beam hit a curtain of falling material – just as before. Whites and pinks and oranges amongst the silt – shapes that hung in front of their eyes like the soft jellies of the deep ocean. Jem gasped at this display. Nick noticed something – the patterns and colours of these objects didn't seem natural. They weren't perfect enough for the living world.

Jem took the mask again and waved for Nick to follow. She shivered, remembering the thing she'd seen eating the riverbed when she first dived in a Black hole. That memory seemed more like a story she'd been told than something she'd actually done. As they hit the bottom, the beam of the torch raked into something metallic. Jem had a sense that the object belonged in the past. They didn't belong here.

Scanning the area with the torch, Nick spotted a rocky shelf – and beyond it, the base of a steel wall – unmistakably man made. Jem tugged at his arm, keen for another gulp of air. As Jem breathed, Nick saw it. A huge shape rising from the dark, bigger than any craft he'd ever seen underwater. Jem motioned towards it – and despite himself, Nick followed. Like pilot fish hugging a shark, the two made their way along the side of the hull, searching for openings.

At last Jem spotted the outline of a round hatchway. A firm twist on the handle and the hatch door opened. Nick followed right behind, pushing himself into the dark space. The chamber on the other side of the door was just big enough for two and altogether dark except for a blue light, somewhere above their heads. Nick flicked on the torch and found the chamber empty except for a steel ladder, reaching upwards towards the faint glow.

Nick drew another breath and handed the mask back. Jem thought about the Angler Fish, a deep sea dweller that lured smaller fish into its jaws with a tiny point of light. She was startled by a sensation behind her. The hatch was closing automatically. Jem shuddered. She longed to check whether the hatch had locked itself behind them but there was barely enough room in the compartment for two. Nick began to climb the ladder, rising towards the glow. Moments later, he emerged squinting into a partially lit chamber that rose high above them. As soon Jem had caught up, he pushed his mask up. The two of them hung like climbers on a steel cliff – with the water echoing through the tank.

89

Water was bubbling through the hatch door at the bottom of the ladder and rushing towards them. Strangely calm, Nick mused on how the waves always chose the shortest possible path to fill the space. Jem tried to climb back down the ladder – forcing herself against the flood.

'Don't bother,' said Nick. 'We're trapped – at least till the pressure in the two rooms has equalized. Even if the outer hatch where we came in isn't locked behind us, we'd never be able to push it open.' Jem stopped climbing down and hauled herself up the ladder with tired arms. At the top of the ladder, Nick had made a discovery. A touch pad was built into the far wall. The keys and screen burned with a faint green light.

'Enter password?' read the prompt. Within a couple of seconds, Jem had pressed every key on the touch pad and was busy wearing out the ENTER button. That approach didn't seem to be working.

'ENTER PASSWORD?' kept coming back like a bad memory.

Jem keyed in the word 'PASSWORD' and hit the ENTER key again. Nothing happened. Below her - the water level was rising fast. Now it was up to her knees. She let out a gulp. Nick shook his head.

'The card,' she screamed. 'What was the message on the card?'

'PRS NTR 2 RLS H20,' remembered Nick. 'We need to key it in exactly though. Do you want me to try? PRS NTR 2 RLS H20.'

Jem took a couple of breaths and keyed in the code exactly as Nick had recited it before hitting the ENTER key again.

'ENTER PASSWORD?' ordered the prompt once again.

'Fill!' screamed Jem, sobbing as the water rose above her hips.

'You must have typed it in wrong or something.'

'No I didn't!' sobbed Jem.

Nick was solving this puzzle with logic – or he would be if it wasn't for the screaming girl next to him. The training course he'd been on mentioned that a firm slap round the face could be justified under certain extreme circumstances, (especially with female subjects, the instructor had added). Nick figured that this situation counted as 'extreme'. He shot his arm back but on second thoughts he grabbed the oxygen mask and thrust it over Jem's mouth, remembering to flick the valve open. With Jem able to breathe air, the compartment was quiet at last. Nick ran the code around and around in his mind as the water rose to neck level. He wasn't even aware of Jem's fingers on the keypad as she hit the key marked ENTER.

The next thing Nick saw was the hatch above them sliding open.

Jem removed the face mask. 'It was easy really. PRS NTR 2 RLS H20. Press the ENTER key to release the H2O. That's water to you, Policeboy. Just press ENTER on its own, no passwords or anything. All the other stuff we were typing was confusing it.'

'Lucky I gave you that oxygen. Good for the brain,' said Nick. As Jem aimed a good slap at Nick's right cheek, she felt her arm caught and twisted in one smooth motion. 'Let go,' she howled. Nick didn't answer. He was looking at a small white duck, which had appeared in the corridor in front of them.

It wasn't the quack of a duck, more of a metallic voice saying 'Quack.'

'Are we hallucinating?' said Nick, imagining the report he'd have to file, and how it would be greeted back at the station boat.

Nick was thinking about hostage situations, where the captives are so shocked that they just follow instructions, go along with whatever the terrorists want them to do. 'What's the matter?' asked Jem. 'Do you think it's luring us back to its terrorist nest?'

'Is this the time for stupid jokes?' snapped Nick.

'Egg-zactly the right time,' said Jem. Why didn't he get that to find something funny, you must first understand it?

'Where are you taking us?' asked the YPD, amazed to find himself talking to a duck.

The duck stopped and turned towards Nick but decided to exercise its right to remain silent. Then Jem approached it:

'Where are you taking us?' demanded Nick. 'Answer me!'

The duck flapped backwards, eyeing the YPD in a wounded way.

'Nice one Policeboy! What are you going to do now? Arrest it? Or threaten to take its eggs into custody?'

'Now you're just being stupid,' said Nick, missing the pun.

'Maybe you've got some beak cuffs on that utility belt of yours?'

'That's enough,' ordered Nick.

The duck turned its back on the forces of law and order and moved off at a slow waddle. There was nothing to do except follow it.

The duck led them through corridor after corridor, eventually arriving at the foot of a long ladder.

'Ha!' said Nick. 'Can't get up eh?' He took a step towards the creature, with a view towards picking it up. Then it flew up the ladder. When the next corridor came to an end, they faced a wall that was bare except for a small pipe. The duck hopped into the pipe and disappeared into the darkness.

It was blacker than a sweep's bath mat down the tunnel. The floor and walls were damp and it stank of something organic. In the total darkness, Jem began to sense that the hole was occupied. As she crawled onwards, she became aware that many small eyes were watching her. At last, the tunnel opened out into a wide open space.

Jem was greeted by a great flapping noise and the swish of webbed feet on water. Bird jostled bird to make way for their unexpected visitor. For a moment she imagined that this was a court and they would be brought for trial before the Swan King – who wanted her hand in marriage or some such.

It was hard for Nick to watch his informer (as he now thought of Jem) disappear down a tunnel. This was the moment that he'd been most afraid of. Now he'd lost control of Jem and the whole situation. He shone his cap light down the tunnel but it didn't get past the first twist before the beam was eaten by the darkness.

Then he heard Jem's voice – it sounded unexpectedly close.

'They've told me to wait here.'

'No!' called Nick. 'You should get back here right now.'

'It said someone's coming. Why stop before the party gets going?'

'Who's coming? 'Is it Father Thames?' 'I need you to ask it!' demanded Nick.

Jem remembered the woodblock print of Father Thames and shivered. If a bearded river demon really did exist, this was exactly the sort of stinking hole that it would hang out in.

'Who's coming?' Jem asked quietly.

'She's coming,' rasped a metallic voice. 'She's coming now.'

40 Watt

Nick got down on his knees and pushed his face into the dark tunnel. There had been no sound for three minutes. He'd timed it using his counting system. For Nick, time never flew, whether he was having fun or not. Nick wasn't having fun right now. In fact he was cursing himself for allowing things to develop like this. Without tools to widen the tunnel, there was no way to follow Jem. Had this been the plan, to separate them? He'd lost control of the situation. Nick was usually his own harshest critic, and would have arrested himself for wasting YPD time. Now Jem was probably being questioned – or if Haig's hunch was right, she'd joined up with her terrorist friends. He cursed himself for making such an entry-level mistake.

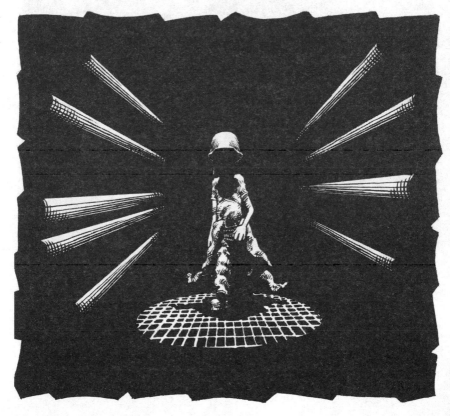

Nick heard the guard's steps long before he could see him. It was tomb quiet except for the sort of humming and droning you'd expect on a secret underwater base. The footsteps were easy to make out. The guard was wearing heavy boots. Nick pressed himself against the wall and thought for a moment. They knew about him, so surprise wasn't going to work here. As the footsteps got louder, the YPD ran back and squeezed his head and upper body into the tunnel. Then he waited. His legs were sticking out of the hole, in plain view.

The guard was a scruffy kid called Asif. He had a face like a robber's horse and he wasn't on the soap seller's Christmas list, judging by the state of his hoodie. The Fatman's nickname for Asif was '40 Watt'. Asif liked the name, thinking it was something to do with speakers. In fact, his boss had named him after the 20th Century's least powerful light bulb. Asif had written it on his helmet. Put simply, Asif was not the brightest star in the midnight sky.

'I've got to bring you with me.'

'I can't. I'm stuck,' said Nick.

'What?' came the question.

'I'm stuck, you'll have to help pull me out.'

There was silence while Asif took this in.

'Grab my boots and give them a pull. I'll try to wriggle free.'

Asif put down his stick and approached the booted feet.

Nick's kick was so strong it nearly bounced the luckless kid off the wall. When Asif came to his senses – his hands were tied, so he didn't notice that his pockets were empty.

The Pool

JEM'S ARRIVAL MADE THE DUCKS SCATTER AND FLAP. Some took off across the pool in a kind of half-run, half swim. Others settled on the delicate scientific equipment scattered around the room. Jem saw the central pool and the nesting areas arranged around it. Three tunnels like the one she'd squeezed down opened out into the pool. A trim woman and a fat man entered by a door at the far end of the chamber. The man, who seemed to be chewing something, was wearing a light green T shirt with nasty brown stains down the front. The neat woman wore a white lab coat.

Jem wondered whether she'd been unfair by blaming the ducks for the smell in here. The man was nursing a tray carefully. 'I'm hungry,' he said. His tray was packed with cakes, fried chicken legs in little paper baskets and all manner of weird food, most of it fried.

The Fatman ignored this remark and threw some bread into the duck pool.

'The male Eiderduck is white and the female is brown,' he whispered. 'See how the male watches the female at all times and anticipates her every need.'

He offered the tray to the woman, who sniffed in disgust.

The Fatman began to throw food into the pool and then grabbed a headset and started shouting into the mike.

'I am the Duck Controller!' rasped a metallic voice.

'You!' gasped Jem. What do you want? What am I doing here?'

'That depends,' said Miss River. 'You're not a child. You're a young woman now and you should be able to make your own mind up.'

The hungry man stopped eating for a moment and looked at Jem as if to make a comment but he stopped short and twiddled with a wire on the headset.

'Black holes! The great unsolved mystery of our times,' he coughed, choking on a hunk of chocolate.

'And the people that go missing near them,' said Jem. She stared intensely at the fat man. One good thing about Jem - she never had a problem with 'intense'.

Hungry for seconds, the ducks began to clamour for more. The Fatman dispensed the food fairly, making sure each one got their share.

'So why do you use the name Father Thames on your cards, if the APD came up with it?' asked Jem. The Fatman looked at Miss River.

'Terrorists – I wouldn't go that far. Maybe, you wouldn't want to leave your houseboat keys with some of them...'

There was a silence, which Miss River filled with a speech which she'd practiced many times in her mind. Now the moment had come she was having trouble striking the right note.

'Look around you Jem. Kids policing other kids, and locking them up in floating prisons. Whilst adults let it slide. One law for the old and another for the young. Does that sound like justice to you?'

'Fight the power Missy!' said the Fatman, pumping one fist in the air whilst guiding another chicken leg towards his throat with the other. Miss River aimed a withering glance at him. Her throat twitched, like it always did when she was seriously angry.

'So it's all a heap of fill,' said Jem. 'And that makes what you're doing right, does it?'

'People living without a simple thing like electricity. Dying from the lack of it.'

'That's how it has to be,' said Jem. 'Since the Flood we've learned to respect the Earth's resources. Didn't you learn anything at school?'

'Get 'em while they're young,' said the Fatman. And he began to do a crazy hand jive, singing, 'Winding the power up, winding the power up, winding the power up today.'

Ignoring him, River continued: 'You decide for yourself Jem.'

'Do you know how much power it takes to run a hospital Jemima?' asked River.

The Fatman flicked a switch and the chamber was awash with intense light. It bounced off the waves in the pool. It reflected and swirled, making tight patterns on the roof. Powerful speakers began to blast out a forgotten tune. 'Blinded by the light...'

'Kill it!' growled River. The Fatman cut the power and the world was dark and quiet again.

'So that's what this place is? A hospital?' asked Jem. 'Great doctors you've got here. All the patients seem to have discharged themselves.'

River smiled. 'We'll talk some more in the morning, if you like.' And with a smile she turned on her heeled boot and left without another word.

'I'm more of an evenings person,' called Jem. 'What exactly do you want from me?' But River clopped off towards the door without looking back.

'Allow me to escort you to your quarters, in the East Wing, m'lady,' said the Fatman. He led Jem through a series of corridors linked by connecting ladders. Plum faced and wheezing, he finally stopped next to a hatch and twisted the handle. 'I've pimped your room. Wide screens. Hi-HD. All kind of disks. Do you like Westerns? John Wayne is the man. Know what I'm saying?'

Jem sighed. She didn't know what he was saying. In fact she could understand about every third word in his last sentence.

'Am I being held here?' asked Jem with tears suddenly in her eyes. The Fatman dropped his remote.

'No,' he said, genuinely surprised. 'Of course not. Do you want to leave?'

Jem thought about it. 'Not yet,' she said,

'Go anywhere you please. Some of the doors are locked but red light spells danger.'

'How can a light spell? sighed Jem.

'It's a figure of speech,' said the Fatman, moving towards the door. 'There are a couple of flooded compartments down here. Open one of them and the pressure would do for us. We'd be mushy peas in a pod.'

'OK,' said Jem.

'Buzz me if you need to know how any of this kit works. Most of it ain't broke but it didn't come with manuals.'

The Gift

'OK Holmes, so what part of 'Go find the YPD kid and call us' didn't you understand?' Laughter from the group of blue-shirted kids rang off the metal walls.

'He said he was stuck,' began Asif.

'Really?'

'In a hole,' said Asif.

'In a hole?' repeated the Fatman, playing to his audience.

'He said to grab his leg and pull him out,' admitted Asif.

'Pull me out man, pull me out innit?' sniggered Shami.

'And then?'

'Then he kicked me,' finished Asif.

'In the head?' laughed Shami, her eyes shone when she giggled.

'The old "pretend to be stuck in a hole" routine?' sighed the Fatman.

'He suckered you,' laughed Jamil.

'Don't you know that's the first thing they teach them at Hendon Marsh? Any trouble, just pretend to be stuck in a hole, ask for help and then kick your opponent in the head!' groaned the Fatman.

'Is it?' asked Asif, as their laugher boomed around the room. He knew that they'd be like this.

'Enough!' said Miss River. Still chocking back the laughter, the Fatman made an immense effort and gave Asif his new orders.

'I guess you'd better make like Burn's spider.'

Asif looked blankly back at him.

'Try again,' said Miss River, helpfully. 'Go and find the YPD. Don't do anything this time, just contact us when you've found him.'

Jamil and Shami nodded. Asif looked puzzled.

'Yes?' asked Miss River.

'Where will you be?' asked Asif.

'We'll be here, 40 watt!' screamed the Fatman. 'Call us on the radio.'

'And be more careful this time,' said Miss River.

'Our YPD is obviously some kind of karate kid, with all of that krazy kicking and stuff. We don't want you coming back all mashed up.'

'Eh?'

'Just call it a gun, 40 watt. This is Quadrophenia model – plenty of cool mods.'

'It can fire underwater right?' asked Asif.

'As if! As if!' howled Jamil.

'That's enough!' ordered River.

'I've made some improvements Asif, but I can't work miracles.'

'Firing is a piece of treacle cake. Wait till you eyeball him. Squeeze to fire. When he's hooked, you squeeze it again to start frying. Then let go of the trigger to cut the juice. Capiche?'

'Do try not to cook each other,' cautioned Miss River.

Asif nodded, lowered the gun and tied his sweat shirt around his waist. The yellow badge on his shirt was faded, but you could still make out writing that said 'C.F.C.' The posse moved off down the corridor, with Asif in the front, brandishing his new toy.

'Please do not shoot anyone unless you absolutely have to,' called Miss River.

'And if you have to shoot, don't miss!' called the Fatman.

'You've only got three shots each before the batteries die,'

Asif and the others swaggered off down the corridor,

'Nothing like a new gun. Puts a spring in a boy's step,' laughed the Fatman.

I Can't Sleep Tonight

JEM WAS FIGHTING SLEEP. Sleep was an experienced warrior. It always won, but Jem could hold out for a while yet. She couldn't help it, but her thoughts kept turning to Nick. Her captors hadn't mentioned him, but Jem guessed that as a YPD, he was in far greater danger than her. Finally, she decided to surrender and turn off the light. Through half shut eyes, points of light winked at her like fireflies. She dreamed that someone was sat down on the end of her bed. She could feel their eyes on her. Jerking upright, she called out a name but the dream figure had gone. Sighing, she put the main light back on and then turned off every one of the Fatman's gadgets, until the room was properly dark. The YPD was on his own now.

Five o' Clock Hero

NICK FELT GREAT, CONSIDERING HE'D HAD BEEN AWAKE FOR 26 HOURS
STRAIGHT. 'Sleep is for sheep,' they used to say back at Hendon Lock.
He still couldn't quite believe how easily the guard had gone down.
Perhaps the terrorists needed to improve their training programme.
His travels around the craft had been equally surprising but also a
little disappointing. There was no sign of weapons, only room after
room of scrap, canned food, barrels and all manner of ancient junk.
The stuff that filled room after room was stacked up in rows. It
included machinery: screens and white boxes. There was paperwork
too, shamefull amounts of hoarded paper.

Nick ploughed on through rooms stacked from floor to ceiling with plastic storage boxes. He hadn't come across any weapons, just rooms full of junk. The most interesting thing he'd found was some heavy machinery, including some huge drill heads. The YPD didn't have time for exploring, he needed to find a safe way to get off the craft, with or without his informer. It was probable that there'd be diving gear somewhere or failing that, he'd have to work out a way to get a signal to the surface. Jem would have been appalled to know that rescuing her was third on his list.

So far he'd found no signs of life and nothing which might help him escape. On a hunch, he tracked back to the machine shop – where he'd seen the drills. Searching the room thoroughly, Nick took in the benches strewn with wires and weird equipment. At last he spotted something familiar: a transmitter device attached

He flicked the switch on and a tiny light began to flash on the remote. It was easy to dial in a YPD frequency where officers would be listening. If only he could get a signal out, they could find him.

Looking around the workshop he noticed that, although grimy,

it was bristling with tools. Nick noticed with approval how the mechanic had sorted all the bolts into different jars according to their size and head type. This was encouraging. Maybe the transmitter could be modified to get a signal out to the surface? After ten wasted minutes exploring this line, he gave up. Of course, he was far too deep, encased by the steel hull of this craft.

Nick's 'hostile situations' training had said 'keep moving to evade capture', apart from when it had said 'hide to evade capture' if it was hopeless. He'd remembered pressing the tutor on this point. How were you supposed to tell when a situation was 'hopeless' if you were in it? The whole idea of the course was a bit of a joke. The YPD didn't practice running away.

Nick stuffed the device into a spare pocket a continued to search the room. It was a fruitless search – there was no sign of the diving gear or air he needed. He cursed himself again for not keeping track of his location on the levels correctly. On an operation like this, a man who couldn't count was as useless as a baby. Just as this thought entered his mind, he felt a stabbing pain in the small of his back.

Tommy

Jᴇᴍ ꜱʜɪᴠᴇʀᴇᴅ, ᴄʟᴜᴛᴄʜɪɴɢ ᴛʜᴇ ʀᴇᴍᴏᴛᴇ ᴄᴏɴᴛʀᴏʟ. The images on the screen were in a grainy black and white, but unmistakable. In an underwater snowstorm, a great curtain was dropping in slow swirls towards the bottom of the river. Through the gloom, Jem saw a figure and shivered. It had a tentacle in its mouth and in its hand it carried a three pronged spear.

'Father Thames?' gasped Jem.

'Just another one of his little helpers,' said the Fatman. 'His name's Tommy. Well, that's not his real name – his real name's Moon actually. Is this what you got me down here to see? You know you've got thirty-two thousand films on disc down here if you're bored.'

'Is this a film that I'm watching? You've got weird taste in movies.'

'Sure have – but this is reality. Follow me, I'll show you.'

Pipeline

Jem stood on a balcony overlooking a pooled area where well-fed ducks paddled and chattered contentedly. The Fatman gulped down a donut as he plugged leads in and out of a rack of equipment.

Watch!' he commanded. An enormous screen, the length of a Hog eye barge, flashed into life. The same image, like snow falling underwater, filled the screens.

Pulling a radio from his pocket, the Fatman held it to his face and keyed the mike: 'Hey mad man Moon, give us a wave will you?'

The familiar figure walked onto camera and waved his trident obligingly. He appeared to have a tentacle, growing from his mouth.

'What's that thing?' gasped Jem.

'Fixed air supply,' explained the Fatman proudly. 'I'm pleased with that – piped air from the ship means he can stay down for much longer. And it beats lugging tanks of air around.'

The Fatman looked over his shoulder.

'Hey Tommy, you got time to bring me back my present?'

'Affirmative Fats, got two units for you. Still sealed.'

'What are you doing?' asked Jem.

The Fatman winked and began to do a little dance.

'We dig dig dig dig dig dig dig the whole day through,' he sang.

'What for?'

'Treasure,' roared the Fatman, like a pirate.

WE'RE MINING THE ANCIENT LANDFILLS FOR A GAS CALLED 'METHANE'.

'What's methane?' asked Jem

The far man let off a loud fart that rang across the room like the blast of a trumpet.

'You disgust me,' said Miss River, stepping away from him.

'Hey. Pardon me. What can I do Doc? I ran out of those charcoal pills you gave me.'

'Methane is a natural gas,' said River. 'With it we can generate electricity. Enough to power whole cities – hospitals, schools, more power than you can imagine.'

Now that this was revealed, she smiled in relief. Now Jem would understand.

'I can imagine a lot of power,' said the Fatman.

'And all for Father Thames?' asked Jem.

'There are great changes to be made. We'll end poverty, change lives, even save them.'

Birds and Wires

NICK FELT THE WIRE ATTACHED TO HIS BACK, AND LOOKED AT THE YOUTH STANDING IN FRONT OF HIM. He waited for the pain to start. The kid stared too, like a puppy who'd caught his first rabbit and didn't know what to do with it.

'Fry him Asif!' 'What are you waiting for?' shouted Jamil.

In a fluid movement Nick rolled towards his attacker, tearing at the wire on his arm. Asif raised the gun again.

Unknown watts of power made every muscle in Nick's body scream. He'd read that you didn't have the breath to cry out when you got shocked like this but he still managed a wail.

Asif lowered the taser, pulled the radio out of the holder and keyed it. Nothing happened – the battery was dead. As Asif wound the radio, Nick saw his chance. His martial arts instructer had once said, 'Pain is the best teacher, but no one wants to go to his lessons.'

Slapping the weapon out of a dazed Asif's hands, Nick rolled through the door and took off down the corridor as fast as his stunned legs could stumble. He'd never encountered this weapon before but he figured that the electric gun could only have a range of a couple of metres if it relied on clamping its target with a wire.

Shami was the first to react – she pushed past the others, out of the hatchway and ran after the YPD.

Rounding the corner, Shami flipped the taser upside down. At the base there was a switch with a somewhat homemade feel to it. One flick and the gun was in 'plasma' mode. The Fatman had modified it so it could fire plasma shells that carried a shock to their target. 'Now *Thomas A. Swift's Electric Rifle* can fry without wires,' he'd said. Shami heard the sound of her steps as she crept down the row. The taser felt heavy in her small palm. The base of the gun was buzzing gently. Shami was charged too. She'd only killed in games before now.

In the room beyond, Nick edged closer to a huddle of ducks, acting as casually as a YPD can with a transmitter in his hand. The pain in his muscles was dying.

Closer he edged, he didn't want to give the birds the impression that he was stalking them. But the long ages of war with the foxes have taught a duck when it is being stalked. They edged backwards and flopped into the pool, preparing to take off. Without warning, Nick launched himself towards the water and grabbed the nearest duck – a beautiful white one, by the neck. Terrified, the bird resisted arrest, flapping for its life. Nick grabbed it and popped the transmitter around its neck. A tiny green light flashed, telling the YPD that his signal was active. At the back of the pool there was a tunnel. This must lead to the outside. So far so good. Now he needed to shoo the duck into the tunnel. When it made the surface, his signal would be picked up by the YPD.

Policing ducks was about as easy as getting Rudi to obey his commands. A racket was needed to shoo these ducks out of the pool into the tunnel. But the craft was quiet, and his attackers must be near. Finally, the white duck surfaced – once again putting its body between the YPD and the group of brown ducks.

'Protecting the girls eh?' called Nick. With a roar he charged into the water, towards the quacking harem. The ducks took off towards the tunnel. When Nick had shoo'd the females inside the tunnel, the lone white male followed on behind them.

Transmission

M<small>ISS</small> R<small>IVER</small> <small>PUT DOWN HER RADIO AND MADE HER EXCUSES.</small>
'I'll be back in five minutes,' she said.

Jem was struggling to make sense of what she'd just heard.

'You can't get power out of a garbage heap. That's fill!'

The Fatman drew closer and spoke in a low whisper.

'Down, deeper and down. Under the riverbed, that's where the dry boys used to bury their garbage in the old days. It was called landfill. Quite Germanic really. LAND FILL.'

'And they used it to get their power?'

'Nope. They just dug a bunch of dirty great holes and filled them up with crud. But a few years later, the crud rots and makes a gas.'

'Like when the dinosaurs died and turned into coal?'

'Yep Holmes. Only quicker. I dig dead things, real good of them to die and deposit their carbon for us.'

'And you're digging it out?' asked Jem.

'Sucking it out,' said the Fatman, making a revolting noise. 'Stick a probe in there followed by a big pipe and suck it out.'

AND IT'S NOT DANGEROUS?

WELL, EVERYTHING HAS IT'S RISKS DIDNT YOU KNOW? OH NO - IT DOESNT ANY MORE. YOU'RE A CHILD OF THE RISKLESS SOCIETY.

'What sort of risks?' demanded Jem angrily.

'Well you might get an escape. Gas escapes to the surface and bubbles the river up a bit.'

'Black holes,' mouthed Jem.

'When a Black hole meets a naked flame – boom!'

Jem had heard enough. She grabbed the first thing that came to hand, which was a remote control unit.

'We're perfecting the process now, we've pretty much fixed it.'

Jem sent the remote control sailing into the middle of the pool. In an instant, a widescreen monitor joined the party. This was followed by a rack of computer equipment – still with a box of donuts on the top. This made the most satisfying splash yet as it was gulped down by the black water.

'Cut that out!' said the Fatman, nicely. Jem didn't.

'Hey, hey!' Mind my phone. Wait wait, not that!'

Jem drew her arm back but paused at the last moment, clutching a disc.

'Anything but that,' pleaded the Fatman.

'What is it? Scientific data?'

'Franco's Chariot,' said the Fatman. 'Sub-prime country punk.'

Jem went on a furious spree of destruction, tearing expensive equipment from the racks and heaving it into the pool.

When the Fatman's desk was clear, she went in search of more things to sink. They weren't hard to find. Nick's training manual would have called this a 'target rich environment.'

Raising his voice for the first time Jem could remember, he shouted:

The Fatman softened at the sight of Jem's tears.

'Give us a break,' he said. 'What do you think we send all of that crud up for before we start the extraction? Hello! Water churning, Black hole getting active. Day trippers please leave the area.'

Jem didn't reply. The tears were streaming down her face. She didn't notice River, quietly entering the room. She was wearing green medical scrubs and surgical gloves.

'We tried to warn you. To get you to move. What do you think those jetskis were all about?'

'I thought they were trying to kill me,' said Jem quietly.

'I have tried to send messages before,' said Miss River. 'Your father intercepted them. That's why I sent the air. It was so expensive, I knew he'd have to let you have it.'

YOU MUST HAVE GUESSED JEM. YOU MUST KNOW BY NOW. JUST LOOK AT THE TWO OF US.

Jem studied their reflections in the glass and held back a gasp. Their fair hair and blue eyes were cast from the same mould.

Miss River put a mothering arm around Jem. It would have been more comforting if the hand wasn't inside a surgical rubber glove.

'Hush now, darling,' she said. 'All this fuss over an old house boat.'

'What about the people disappearing, Mother?' asked Jem coldly. 'Is that Father Thames work too?'

'That is nothing to do with us – I promise,' said Miss River.

'She's damn right,' said the Fatman. 'Ask your little YPD

'Please stop crying darling,' said Miss River.

'You say I'm free? OK. I'm going,' sobbed Jem.

'You've had twelve years of lies Jem, I've only had a few hours with you.'

'I want to go now, please,' said Jem flatly. The Fatman, looking somehow leaner, shrugged his shoulders.

'Come with me,' said Miss River, there's something I have to finish first, and then you can go.'

You Really Got Me

THE NEXT THING NICK SAW WAS SHAMI, AT THE FAR END OF THE CHAMBER. As Nick edged slowly back around the pool, he struggled to remember his weaponry course. Every weapon has its weakness, the instructor had said. This electric weapon needed wires to carry its charge. As long as he kept away from his attacker, it was useless. Its only threat was fear, from the memory of the pain it had caused.

Nick looked at Shami in disbelief. 'Wait!' he said, 'I give up.'

His eyes never left the girl as he waded towards the side. A stunned duck bobbed lifelessly, till Nick clipped it and brought it back to life. It started to flap and gave out a little cry.

'Don't try anything Piggy,' shouted Shami from the poolside.

Nick picked up the injured duck, cradling it in his hands.

The struggle was brief. Nick used his full weight to keep her head under water for long enough to disarm her. Later, Asif found her cuffed to the pool ladder, with her gun and battery pack gone.

I Can't Explain

'HOLD HER TIGHTLY,' SAID MISS RIVER. Jem held the struggling duck as her mother eased its dislocated wing into a splint. Her fingers worked fast and skillfully, easing the bandage into place. When it was done, Miss River gently set it down on a bed of fresh straw.

Machinery

He had followed the hum down to the engine room. Now he stood in awe before the shaft that drove the sub's twin propellers. Those old screws only knew one way to go. They didn't have any doubts to stop them turning.

Nick wasn't at all sure he should be doing this. Disabling the engine was the correct move, in theory. But he'd had no luck on this mission. Good fortune never came easy, it was as if some greater power was pulling the strings. No wonder the 'sadistic design' theory was catching on amongst the 'Dults. Nick wasn't about to start burning offerings just yet. Now it was down to force - blind and simple. He had to disable the engine, so that the craft would be forced to the surface.

Nick raised the gun, closing his eyes as he squeezed and fired. The cloud of charged plasma gas turned the steel a hazy blue but the prop chugged on, keen as ever. Nick's curse was drowned by the drone of the engine. This was it. Well - not quite, but he knew he only had two shots left. He inched towards the spinning shaft, as if approaching a sleeping dragon. Warm air from the turning steel blasted into his face. It was madness to get this close. Turning his head away from the spinning metal, he raised the weapon and squeezed the trigger again.

The Sky is Crying

'DID YOU FEEL THAT?' called the Fatman, spinning on his leather executive chair and nearly spilling his chocolate shake.

'Getting a little bumpy for you?' cracked Tommy, over the radio.

'Bumpy, my gut!' said the Fatman. 'We've lost all power. You got enough air to surface?'

'Nope,' said the diver, cheerily.

'Well I hope you're a fast swimmer. You'd better dust your broom and get back here, cos we're headed down.'

'Report please?' said Miss River over the intercom.

'Status: panic. We've just lost all power to the engines.'

'Is that a quote from Space Race? Have you've been watching 80's TV again?' said River.

'One more thing. Jem will be leaving us, for now' said River. 'I thought Tommy could escort her to the surface in the mini sub.'

'No one's escorting anyone. We've all got an appointment with old man riverbed, unless we fix the engines.'

'Understood.' said River.

We Are Not Free

THE FATMAN PRISED AT THE CHARRED COVER OF A CONTROL PANEL WITH HIS FRUIT KNIFE. The knife hadn't seen much fruit action - but the Fatman had the touch of an expert. He popped the cover off to reveal the charred insides, leaking smoke.

'Is it mental weakling's week or something?' screamed the Fatman. 'You'd better deal with it, kids.'

Shami nodded.

'Here,' said the Fatman handing her a tazor.

'Thanks,' nodded Shami. 'No worries. It's 'buy-one-get-one-free on plasma guns this week.'

'One more thing,' said the Fatman as they got ready to leave.

'Teachers say that kids need freedom to fail,' said the Fatman. 'Just don't start now, as failure may lead to death by drowning!'

River and Jem entered the great chamber just in time to catch this last remark. River rolled her eyes and sighed, saying nothing.

'I could go with them,' said Jem. 'The YPD's a bit of an idiot but he might listen to me.'

'That won't be necessary,' said Nick, stepping out from his hiding place, the tazor leveled at them. 'You know what to do.' Shami and Jamil lowered their weapons.

'You as well Fats!'

'Nice to meet you too,' said the Fatman. 'And this is a soldering iron, for fixing stuff. It's not even hot.'

'Throw it down,' ordered Nick.

'Sure. But one thing you need to know. Engine stops turning, no power to control the gas flow. Gas comes out of hole too fast – boom, boom, boom.'

'He's telling the truth, I heard them talking before,' said Jem. Nick held Jem's gaze for as long as he dared. Was she a part of this? He wasn't sure.

Nick did the exact opposite, aiming the weapon at the Fatman's face and stroking the trigger.

'Get on with the repairs,' he ordered.

The Fatman stopped, looking up at Nick.

'Hey officer,' said the Fatman, slowly standing up. 'Don't shoot things you don't understand.' Suddenly, the Fatman had found plenty of presence. He was fat like an oak tree - his soft form had gone all solid. He fixed the YPD with a challenging stare, like a bear about to try its claws on a sapling. Extending a chubby hand, palm out, he said: 'I'll need that.'

Nick knew he couldn't surrender the weapon. But shooting the only man who could repair the ship wasn't the smart option either. He noticed a couple of pressure suits hung by a rack of gear.

'Forget swimming out,' said the Fatman. 'We're too deep. Shoot me and we'll all go down together.'

'Something is bothering me,' exclaimed Jem, as if she was the host at a dinner party where one of the guests had chosen an unfortunate topic and she needed to move things on.

'If there's all of this wonderful gas down here, just waiting to be piped out, why don't the YPD just take it out and use it?'

'They won't,' said River.

'Why not?' asked Jem

'They daren't dig the river's heart,' said River.

'Not here,' began River. 'But what about the rest of the planet? Or don't they count as people? They were born poor and they'll die fast, without harming your precious environment?'

'Spare me the rant please,' said Nick, pointing the gun at River.

'There is ample power out there Jem,' continued River. 'But the YPD are too busy imprisoning other kids to use it.'

'I blame the parents,' said the Fatman. 'As ye reap, so shall ye sow.' With the final word, he jabbed the hot soldering iron into Nick's weapon hand. Nick had already squeezed the trigger before he smelled his own skin burning. The plasma gun discharged with a blast and the fat man crashed like a felled oak. Jamil and Shami rushed forward screaming and piled onto Nick, knocking him down. Asif began to stamp on him, twisting his foot as if he was putting out a cigarette.

'That's enough!' ordered River. The three obediently stopped. River picked up the gun and set it down on the console.

Asif stepped over Nick and approached the Fatman, whose body was twitching slightly and went to stroke his head.

'What now?' asked Jem.

'I'll help him,' said River, opening a medical pack. She glared at Nick, shaking. Then she answered the question before Jem asked it.

'You'd better go.'

'Er, okay,' said Jem, 'but how?'

'There's a mini sub on the deck above us. Hatch 11.'

'He'll be all right, won't he?' asked Jem.

River looked at Jem, and then turned her eyes to Nick, shaking with rage. 'Just go!' cried River. 'He warned me not to try. I never listened,' she said, the tears finally coming.

'It's done now,' cried Shami. 'You and the Piggy better run!'

Precious

Tears streaked down Jem's face as the mini-sub rose gently through the bubbles to the river's surface. Nick offered her a comforting arm. And for the first time in her life, Jem didn't reject it.

Hendon Marsh

RUDI CRASHED INTO HIS MASTER'S ROOM, WAGGING HIS TAIL FRANTICALLY. In a quick circuit of the room, he scattered Jem's few possessions and most of Nick's stuff too. The tiger clock fell off the wall with a crash that made the big Alsatian yelp. Jem patted his head. 'Never mind,' she said. 'Your master said I have to take that down anyway.' At Hendon Marsh, where the YPD trained their new recruits, there were rules about what you could have on your walls.

Jem stroked the dog's head again and poured some fresh water into his bowl. Rudi stepped into the bowl, spilling half the water, still wagging his tail. The training at Hendon Marsh was the toughest thing that Jem had ever taken on, but it was a part of the deal she'd cut with Haig. It was quite an eye opener – the baby faced thug was a different character once you were inside the YPD. He was the sort of player you wanted to have on your team. Haig had tried to hide it, but he was impressed by Nick's reports of how Jem had handled herself on her first operation. Putting Father Thames out of action at last been a real acheivement. Nick had been great too. Really supportive.

Rudi bounded to the window, sending more things flying. Paws on the window ledge, he looked out over the shanty town towards the peaceful blue of the Thames. There was nothing unusual to see, just a sailboat sliding by. The crew were busy hauling at the ropes, singing questionable songs. An unexpected gust filled the sails and the white sheets began to flow as they caught the wind. On one of the broken-down rooftops, far below Jem's window, Rudi didn't notice what had been waiting ever so patiently – one small white duck.

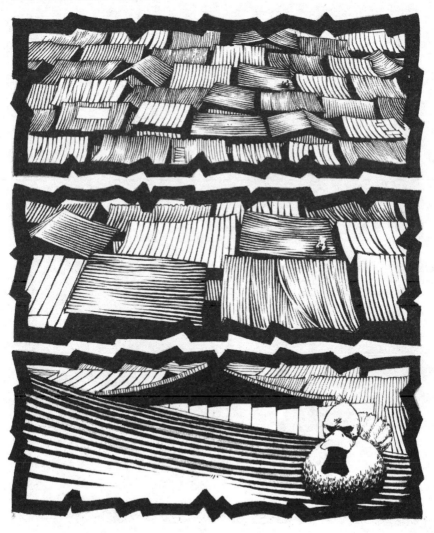

In Volume 2 of 'London Deep'...

Father Thames goes to war.

FATHER THAMES

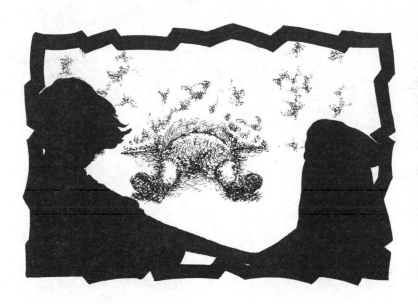

MOGZILLA

HAYWIRED
By Alex Keller

In the quiet village of Little Wainesford, Ludwig von Guggenstein is about to have his unusual existence turned inside out. When he and his father are blamed for a fatal accident during the harvest, a monstrous family secret is revealed. Soon Ludwig will begin to uncover diabolical plans that span countries and generations while ghoulish machines hunt him down. He must fight for survival, in a world gone haywire.

ISBN: 978-1-906132-33-0
UK: £7.99

http://www.mogzilla.co.uk/haywired

Also by Robin Price:

I AM SPARTAPUSS

In the first adventure in the Spartapuss series...
Rome AD 36. The mighty Feline Empire rules the world.
Spartapuss, a ginger cat is comfortable managing Rome's finest
Bath and Spa. But Fortune has other plans for him. Spartapuss
is arrested and imprisoned by Catligula, the Emperor's heir. Sent
to a school for gladiators, he must fight and win his freedom in
the Arena - before his opponents make dog food out of him.

'This witty Roman romp is history with cattitude.'
Junior Magazine (Scholastic)

ISBN 13: 978-0-9546576-0-4

UK £6.99
USA $14.95/ CAN $16.95

http://www.mogzilla.co.uk/spartapuss

CATLIGULA

In the second book in the Spartapuss series, history takes a terrible turn for the worse as Catligula becomes Emperor. Rome's new ruler is mad, bad and dangerous to stroke. When Spartapuss starts a new job at the Imperial Palace, he is horrified to find that Catligula wants him as his new best friend. The Spraetorian Guard plot to tame the power-crazed puss before he ruins the Empire. But will Spartapuss play ball?

Cat-tastic!' - *London Evening Standard*

ISBN: 9780954657611

UK £6.99
USA $14.95/ CAN $16.95

http://www.mogzilla.co.uk/spartapuss

DIE CLAWDIUS

In the third installment of the series, six-clawed hero
Spartapuss is horrified to find that the Emperor is planning an
invasion of the Land of the Kitons, aka Great Britain.
Clawdius, the least likely emperor in Roman history, needs to
show his enemies who is boss. While Spartapuss has always
wanted to visit his birthplace--famous for its terrible food, evil
weather, and the tuneless howling of its savage tribes--he is
loath to journey there as part of an invasion. However, he soon
finds himself rounded up and forced aboard the first ship in
the invasion fleet and part of the landing party that sets out
to search for the Kiton Army. Soon captured by two warriors,
Spartapuss manages to escape into the woods, where he
meets Furg, a young Kiton studying to become a Mewid. After
joining her at Mewid training school, Spartapuss realizes he
must choose between his new friends and the Emperor. Can
the magic of the Mewids help him make the right decision?

Another fantastic story in this brilliantly inventive
series!' - *Teaching and Learning Magazine*

ISBN: 9780954657680

UK £6.99
USA $14.95/ CAN $16.95

http://www.mogzilla.co.uk/spartapuss

BOUDICAT

Rome AD 36. The mighty Feline Empire rules the world. Queen Boudicat has declared war on Rome and wants Spartapuss to join her rebel army. Our ginger hero can't see how a tiny tribe of Kitons can take on the mighty Feline Empire. But warrior queens don't take 'No' for an answer. Boudicat is not for turning, she's for burning!

Action-packed and full of historical details, the Spartapuss series follows the diary of a gladiator cat from Rome to the Land of the Kitons (A.K.A. Britain). Boudicat, the fourth book in the Spartapuss series, was awarded an 'Exclusively Independent' pick of the month for July 2009.

"An exciting series... really good books. I would recommend them to 10 year olds and upwards who enjoy thrillers that you can't put down 'til you've read the whole thing!" – Flora Murray, Dalry Secondary School S1, *The Journal of Classics Teaching*

ISBN: 9781906132019

UK £5.99

http://www.mogzilla.co.uk/spartapuss

CLEOCATRA'S KUSHION

In the fifth exciting *Spartapuss* adventure, the Son of Spartapuss visits Rome and falls in love with a female with the most beautiful name he has ever heard. He invites the fair Haireena on a date to the Emperor's unfinished Golden Palace, but things soon get out of hand. The pair are discovered by the cruel emperor Nero, who decides that Haireena will make the perfect present for his favourite gladiator.

After breaking out of Hades Row, (Rome's Worst Prison), SOS chases the gladiator only to find that he's taken Haireena on a secret mission in search of a treasure cavern at the source of the river Nile. Their journey to the Kingdom of the Kushites is full of shocks, crocs and a touch of magic, courtesy of Cleocatra's Kushion.

Coming in April 2011
ISBN: 978-1-906-132-06-4

UK: £7.99

http://www.mogzilla.co.uk/spartapuss